James Miln

Excavations at Carnac - Brittany

A record of archaeological researches in the Bossenno and the Mont Saint Michel

James Miln

Excavations at Carnac - Brittany
A record of archaeological researches in the Bossenno and the Mont Saint Michel

ISBN/EAN: 9783337336059

Printed in Europe, USA, Canada, Australia, Japan

Cover: Foto ©Andreas Hilbeck / pixelio.de

More available books at **www.hansebooks.com**

EXCAVATIONS

AT

CARNAC

(BRITTANY)

A RECORD OF ARCHÆOLOGICAL RESEARCHES IN

THE BOSSENNO

AND THE MONT SAINT MICHEL

BY

JAMES MILN

EDINBURGH

DAVID DOUGLAS, No. 9 SOUTH CASTLE STREET

MDCCCLXXVII.

Printed by R. & R. CLARK, *Edinburgh.*

PREFACE.

In the summer of 1873 I went on a tour in Brittany for the purpose of seeing some of the antiquities for which it is so famous, my chief object being to visit the celebrated alignments of Carnac.

Landing at St. Malo, I proceeded by the beautiful scenery of the Rance to Dinan, and thence on to Morlaix. There a few days were pleasantly passed in making excursions to visit the curious churches and calvaries of St. Thegonnec and St. Guimiliau, and in examining the houses of the fifteenth, sixteenth, and seventeenth centuries, which are still to be seen in the Grande Rue, and in the Rue des Nobles at Morlaix. These picturesque specimens of Breton architecture usually present their gable ends to the street, each successive storey projecting over the one below it, and they are often adorned with quaint carving on the woodwork.

Proceeding onwards and making short stoppages at Brest, Pleybe, Quimper, Concarneau, Pontaven, and Quimperle, I eventually arrived at Auray, where carriages can always be obtained for Carnac.

Shortly after my arrival at Carnac, my attention was drawn to the Mounds of the Bossenno by a French archæologist,

who stated that he had discovered and intended to excavate
them. In the end of the summer of 1874 he renounced his
intention, and I then undertook the work, which I super-
intended and carried on at my own expense. On becoming
better acquainted with Carnac and its surrounding country,
I found that these Mounds were perfectly well known by
the name of "Cæsar's Camp," that they had long attracted
the attention of antiquaries, and had been mentioned in
archæological works, though no attempt had been made to
ascertain their true character by systematic excavations.

Foreseeing the advantages to be derived from possessing
the ground occupied by the Mounds of the Bossenno, I
endeavoured to purchase it, but difficulties too numerous
to mention compelled me to abandon the idea. Had I
succeeded, many difficulties as to obtaining permission to
excavate would have been obviated, and much expense in
carting away the excavated materials would have been saved,
as the stones could then have been utilised in constructing
a wall round the ruins, so as to preserve them from injury.

There still remains much to be done at the Bossenno to
complete the excavations described in the following chapters,
and I may perhaps continue these excavations if the necessary
permission can be obtained.

In compliance with the wishes of friends in France, the
description of the excavations of the Bossenno was first written
and printed in French. Every one knows the difficulties
and disadvantages of writing in a foreign language; I
therefore had recourse to my friend the Count de Martel,
and to M. le Men, Archéviste of Quimper, to whom I am

indebted for revising the text of the French edition. I am also indebted to M. Paul Gervais, Professor of the Museum of Natural History, Paris, for classifying the bones, and to M. H. Cohen, Attaché of the Bibliothèque Nationale, for classifying the coins found at the Bossenno.

The wood engravings in this work have been executed by M. Emile Nicolay; the pottery is mostly produced from drawings by MM. Henri Du Cleuziou and Louis Cappé; while the plans, landscapes, and statuettes are from my own drawings. Although the woodcuts introduced as vignettes at the end of the several chapters in the text of this volume have no direct bearing on the excavations at the Bossenno, the objects thus represented are generally remarkable for their local or special characteristics. Amongst these I may notice the Lech at Plouharnel, as an example of a peculiar class of sepulchral monument, believed by many antiquaries to be the intermediate link between the ancient unsculptured menhir and the sculptured headstone of later times.

I have much pleasure in expressing my obligations to the clergy and the authorities for their kind offices, to the proprietors of the ground for their permission to excavate, and to the worthy proprietress of the Hôtel des Voyageurs at Carnac for placing all the resources of that well-known establishment at my disposal throughout my stay at Carnac.

CONTENTS.

IV.—MOUND C.

V.—MOUND D.

VI.—MOUND E.

XI.—MONT ST. MICHEL.

LIST OF ILLUSTRATIONS.

3.—MOUND B.

4.—MOUND C.

5.—MOUND D.

6.—MOUND E.

7.—MOUND F.

I.

THE BOSSENNO.

B

ENVIRONS OF CARNAC.

FROM THE "CARTE ARCHÉOLOGIQUE DU MORBIHAN," BY ED. BASSET.

To face page 3.

THE BOSSENNO.

THE little town of Carnac, situated in the Department of the Morbihan, about nine miles to the south of Auray, is visited by numerous travellers from all parts of the world, attracted thither by the celebrity of its alignments and other stone monuments.

In following the road from Auray to Carnac, a striking difference is observed in the appearance of the country. In approaching the coast the land becomes less fertile ; on every hand sterile tracts of moorland appear, on which stand the monuments called Celtic, viz. menhirs,* dolmens,† and tumuli, all of which become more numerous within a mile of Carnac.

The traveller's first impressions, however, are not favourable ; the country seems flat and uninteresting, and his expectations are not immediately realised. It is only after he has remained some time at Carnac, and become more intimately acquainted with the surrounding country, that he begins to appreciate the number, extent, and variety of the Celtic monuments and Gallo-Roman ruins with which it is studded, and to realise that the time thus devoted to the examination of these in detail has been amply repaid.

* Men-hir, from the Breton *Men*, a stone, and *hir*, long—literally a long stone.

† Dol-men, from the Breton *Dol*, a table, and *men*, a stone—literally a stone table.

According to Cæsar's *Commentaries* this country was in-habited before the Roman Conquest by the Veneti, the most powerful people of Armorica.

Its occupation by the Romans until the year 409, that is for more than four centuries, must of necessity have left very marked traces of the masters of the world. These are to be seen in the numerous Gallo-Roman ruins which have been explored of late years, and in the Roman tiles and pottery which are so frequently met with in traversing the fields. During all this lapse of time the country was inhabited (accord-ing to the Roman authors) by a population who had in a large measure adopted the manners and customs of the Romans.

It is especially on the sea-coast of Armorica that the juxta-position of Celtic monuments and Gallo-Roman ruins attracts the attention of the observer, and suggests questions of what had led to this juxtaposition of monuments whose origin is so different. This question is an interesting one. Without pre-tending to solve it, I may be permitted to cite a few places where this proximity may be easily verified. At Locmariaker, Roman ruins are found alongside of the Celtic monuments; at Kerilio, in Erdeven, the same may be seen in the sandy downs to the south of the village; at Carnac, the Roman ruins of the Bossenno are surrounded by Celtic monuments.

It is owing to explorations which have been made, during the last thirty or forty years, by the different Archæological Societies in Brittany, and also by private individuals, that numerous Gallo-Roman establishments have been discovered in that province. This is a proof of the progress of archæo-logy in Brittany, for at that time several antiquaries held that the Romans had never penetrated to the extreme point of Armorica.

The *Transactions* of the Polymathic Society of the Mor-

THE ALIGNMENTS OF MENHIRS AT KERMARIO

TAYLOR

bihan, for 1857, contain reports on the exploration of the following Gallo-Roman establishments :—

At St. Christophe, in the Commune of Eloen—description of the explorations, and plan. At Lodo, in the Commune of Arradon—description, plan, drawings of objects found, and account of Roman coins collected. At St. Symphorien, near Vannes—description and plan.

In the Department of Finistère there has also been discovered, at Parc-en-Croix, near Quimper, a Gallo-Roman military post, of which there is a description and plan in the third volume of the *Transactions* of the Archæological Society of Finistère.

At Poulker, near the embouchure of the Odet, on the left bank of the river of Quimper, Gallo-Roman ruins were explored in 1866, for the Archæological Society of Finistère, by M. le Men, Archéviste of the Department.

M. Fornier has also published a description and plans of his explorations at Haut-Beeherel, in the Commune of Corseul (Coté du Nord).

Numerous other discoveries might easily be cited, but it would be superfluous to do so, since Gallo-Roman remains have been found almost everywhere in Brittany, thus proving that Armorica was occupied as long and as fully as the other parts of Gaul.

Amongst the number of unexplored Gallo-Roman remains in the Department of the Morbihan several works on archæology mention certain mounds* called "Cæsar's Camp," situated a mile to the east of Carnac, and near the village of Cru-Carnac, their origin being indicated by the fragments of Roman

---

* Amongst others, the *Repertoire Archéologique du Morbihan*, published by M. Rozenweig. These mounds had also been pointed out to several archæologists by M. Charles de Kerenflech-Kevegne before 1860.

tiles strewn on their surface. Shortly after my arrival at
Carnac in 1873 these mounds were pointed out to me ; and
the more I saw of them, the more I desired to explore them.

These mounds are situated in the following portions of the
section M, second subdivision of the Cadastre.*

No. 610. Er Vurten.	No. 649. Bossenno.
„ 611. Boceno.	„ 651. Bocenneu.
„ 612. Boceno Hir.	„ 652. Bocenneu.
„ 647. Clos Gurunne.	

These portions of land form part of an elevated plateau,
extending from them towards the sea.

The etymology of the word Bossenno appears to show
that it is derived from the Breton word *bossen* (a mound or
heap) in the plural *boceno, bossenno,* or *bocenneu,* according to
the different dialects. This etymology of the word is in
harmony with the character of the objects to which the name
is given, consisting of a cluster of mounds occupying an area
which may be estimated at 6578 square yards.

Commencing at 200 yards to the east of the village of
Cru-Carnac, this area extends eastward to the edge of the
valley now called *Ker-ine-goh,* but in the old titles of 1740,
Ker-guin-goh.† These old titles will be hereafter alluded to
as proving that the sea came up to Ker-guin-goh during the
last century.

A talus of unequal dimensions stretches along the north

---

* See the general plan of the Bossenno.

† This word signifies the old town of Guen, or the town of Old Guen.
A curious old cross, figured at the end of this chapter, is situated about 500
yards to the north-west of Ker-guin-goh. It is named Croaz-ar-Guen. The
Breton word *guen* or *van,* or *ban* in the Celtic, signifies white. Guened is
the town of Vannes, and Guenedi the Veneti. The most common names of
the inhabitants of the village of Cru-Carnac are Guen-ac (whites), and
Baelagu (priests).

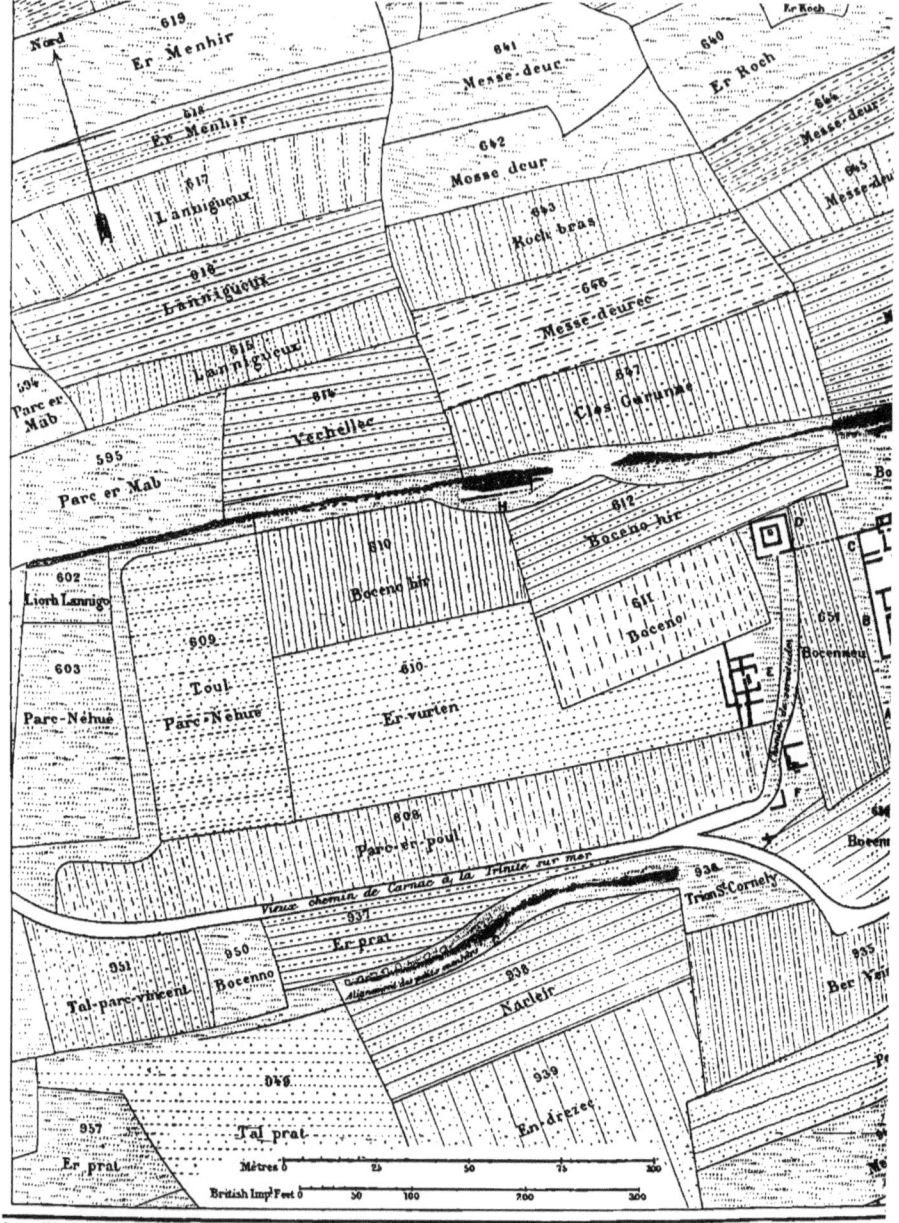

James Miln fecit.

To face page 6.

GENERAL PLAN

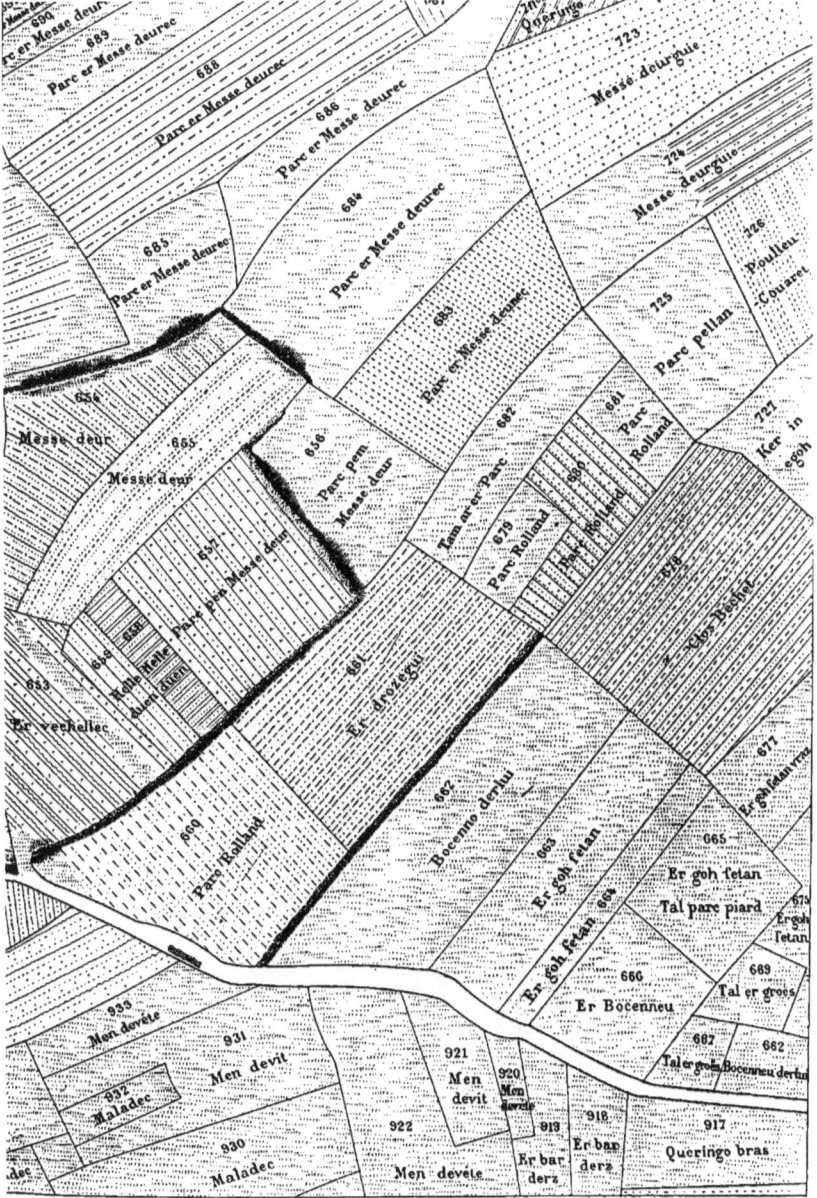

side of this ground, and appears in some parts also on the south side. When making several trenches across the northern talus, I found the remains of a wall measuring 5 ft. in breadth and 5 ft. in height, built with large undressed stones without lime, similar in its masonry to the walls of the Middle Ages.

From the commencement of the work at the Bossenno, this talus seemed to me to have been an *enceinte*, and the discovery of the stone wall strengthened this impression. This destination is also indicated by the difference of level between the north and south sides of the talus : on the north side the ground is fully three feet lower ; and this leads me to suppose that on this side a moat had been cast, the earth from which had served to heighten the *enceinte*.

The legends of a country are never to be overlooked, especially when they bear upon the researches in which one is engaged.

The group of mounds called the Bossenno have their legend, and it has a certain analogy with certain facts which the excavations there have brought to light. The tradition of the country is that the Bossenno were inhabited by the red monks (the Templars) who, having exasperated the country by their crimes, drew down upon themselves a terrible punishment, their neighbours having killed them and burnt their habitations in one night. It will be afterwards seen that in the exploration of the ruins of the Bossenno the unmistakable proofs were everywhere found of their having been destroyed by fire.

These mounds have an evil reputation to this day. The peasants tell you "those who pass by them late at night may happen to see each mound illuminated, and sometimes to hear an animated conversation, of which not a word can be understood, for it is in Latin."

The exploration of the Bossenno was commenced in the beginning of September 1874. The excavation of each separate mound was undertaken successively. Each of the mounds so excavated is distinguished in the general plan by a particular letter. Up to this time eight mounds have been explored, and these are distinguished in the following pages by the letters A, B, C, D, E, F, G, H.

I shall confine myself principally to the description of the constructions found under the respective mounds, with an enumeration of the objects collected from them, reserving for the concluding chapter a few remarks regarding the special nature of these constructions, and the time when they had been destroyed.

CROAZ-AR-GUEN.

II.

EXCAVATIONS IN THE MOUND A.

THE MOUND A.

THE excavations at the Bossenno were commenced in the early part of September 1874, on the mound indicated in the general plan by the letter A. It was one of the smallest of several artificial eminences in the field 649 Bossenno, of which it occupied the south end. In form it was a low circular mound, having a height of about 3 feet, and a circumference at the base of about 130 feet.

Before proceeding farther, it may be as well to indicate the method which was followed in conducting the diggings, not only of this mound, but of those successively explored.

The different objects brought to light by the labours of the workmen—such as bricks, tiles, pottery, metals, bones, etc. —were carefully laid aside. The fragments of pottery and tiles were first of all submitted to a preliminary examination, with the view of finding the potters' marks or names. At the end of each day the more interesting objects were carried to the Hotel des Voyageurs at Carnac, where they were submitted to a more careful examination, previous to being classed and ticketed, so that no errors might occur as to the precise position in which they had been found.

The workmen commenced digging on the south side of the mound, and were not long in turning up a quantity of debris, consisting of fragments of Roman roofing tiles (*Tegulæ* and *Imbrices*), also sundry fragments of Gallo-Roman pottery in red, gray, and black ware. After several hours' work we came upon the outside of the north wall.

Here some unforeseen difficulties arose, which stopped the work for several days. The lessee of the grazing of the field set up a claim for indemnity which he had not previously required, and which ultimately had to be submitted to. On the other hand, the proprietor raised a still greater difficulty by exacting that all the excavated stones and rubbish should be carted away clear of his fields. Thanks, however, to the kind intervention of Dr. de Gressy and of M. Broux, the Mayor of Carnac, leave was obtained to deposit these on the waste land below Kercado, about a mile distant from the Mound A, and upon some parts of the old road which traverses the Bossenno towards the Trinité-sur-Mer. As soon as these arrangements were concluded, the diggings were immediately resumed.

The outside of the wall previously mentioned was followed by cutting a trench along it lengthways down to its foundation. Several days were passed in carrying this trench round the outside of the dwelling so long buried under the Mound A. When finished it exposed a building of quadrilateral form, each of its sides measuring nearly 34 feet, excepting that on the south, which was somewhat less than the others. This irregularity of construction is not uncommon in Gallo-Roman buildings.

The walls measured 2 feet in breadth, and were constructed with small cubic stones, carefully laid, and bedded in lime mortar. Some of the neighbouring peasants who came to see the diggings were much astonished at the regularity of the courses of small cubic stones, and remarked as well that

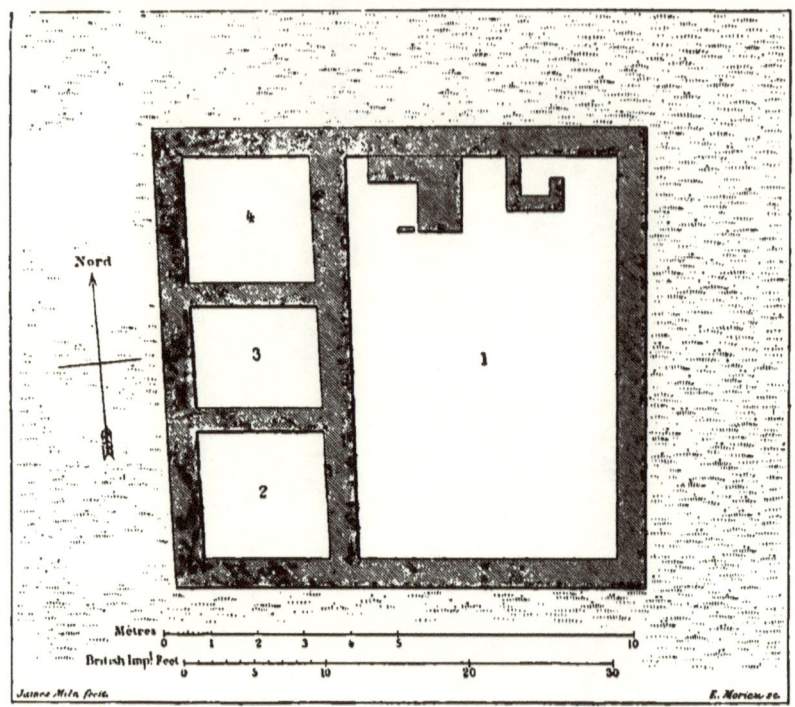

A, PLATE I.—PLAN OF THE BUILDING.

the breadth of the walls was the same as in the modern buildings in the environs of Carnac.

The following days were employed in clearing out the interior of the building. The result of this was to expose a dwelling of four rooms, of which I shall now give the description, designing each by the number it bears on the plan A, plate I.

No. 1.—This apartment, by far the largest, measured 28 feet by 18, and occupied all the east side of the house. Two pieces of masonry projected from the inner side of the north wall, and marked the places which had been occupied by two constructions, whose remains were now so dilapidated as to afford no definite indication of their original destination. It was, nevertheless, agreed by all who saw them, that they might have been furnaces.

Nos. 2 and 3.—The first of these rooms formed a square, measuring 9 feet on each side. The second measured 9 feet by 7 feet.

The flooring of the rooms 1, 2, and 3, was formed of a thick layer of concrete cement.

No. 4.—This room was also square, and measured 9 feet on each side. It had been paved with square tiles, but these were found displaced and broken. Other fragments of tiles were collected here, which were ornamented with diagonal lines and concentric circular markings. Subsequent experience showed that these tiles had been sometimes used for decorative purposes, while in other cases the hollow lines had served to make the plaster adhere. Three paving tiles were found which bore the impression of the feet of dogs, which had passed over them when the clay was in the soft state.

The floors of these four rooms, which have just been described, were covered with a layer of cinders, charcoal, and ashes, mingled with pieces of iron, scoriæ, and even of granite vitrified. The impression derived from the presence of these objects, and from the consideration of other circumstances revealed during the progress of the diggings, was that the building had been destroyed by fire, while the quantity of broken pottery* found within its precincts renders it probable that the dwelling had been previously pillaged; for it is proverbial that the marauder destroys all that he is unable to appropriate or does not care to carry away.

After the four rooms had been entirely cleared out, trenches were dug across the floor of the room No. 1 from north to south, and also all round the base of the walls of the building on the inside.

At a depth of 12 inches under the floor the workmen came upon a layer, 4 inches thick, composed of bones of ruminants, shells of edible molluscs, ashes, cinders, charcoal, and fragments of pottery. Another bed of the same nature was found 22 inches lower still. These two layers seemed to be the evidences of two burnings anterior to that which had destroyed the house buried under the Mound A. An apparent corroboration of this view is found in the fact that, as we got deeper down in the trenches, the forms of the pottery became more simple, and showed only plain edges.

The debris which was carted away from the inside of the building, was composed principally of small cubic building stones, fragments of flat roofing tiles (*Tegulæ*) and of ridge tiles (*Imbrices*). From all this quantity of debris, however, there were only extracted entire one flat roofing tile and six ridge tiles. Subsequently, when exploring the other mounds of the Bossenno, a considerable number of both *Tegulæ* and

* For detailed descriptions of the pottery, see pp. 18-24.

2

3   E.N.   1

To face page 15.   A, PLATE II

Imbrices were found entire, so that I was enabled to reconstruct a portion of the roof, which was deposited and may be
seen in the newly-formed museum in the Mairie of Carnac,
and where, it is to be hoped, that it will remain after the ruins
of the Bossenno have entirely disappeared.*

The following is a descriptive list of the most important
objects found in clearing out the inside of the buildings :—

Several large pieces of querns or hand-mills in granite and
conglomerate or " pudding stone," reddened by the action of fire,
were found scattered on the floor of the room No. 1.

Part of a broken implement in yellow sandstone, cut in
facets, polished by use.   This appeared to have been a hone
or sharpening stone.   (A, pl. II. fig. 3.)

Several fragments of implements in gray slate polished by
use, which appeared to have been used as rubbing stones or
burnishers.   (A, pl. II. fig. 1.)

Several worked flakes of black flint similar to the flint of
the English Channel as found near Dieppe.

An implement in gray flint unpolished, and measuring
4½ inches by 3 inches.   (A, pl. II. fig. 2.)

Mr. Le Guennec, proprietor of the field in which the mound
A was situated, discovered, when removing the ruins of a
dolmen from one of his fields a few years ago, a stone axe also
in gray flint and of the same form as that here described.
Mr. Le Guennec placed his axe in the museum, in the Mairie
of Carnac.   The dolmen in which it was found was situated
in a meadow field near the village of Kerfraval, distant about
half a mile to the south of the Bossenno.

* A few years ago there was discovered near Redon, in the grounds belonging to the Eudiste fathers of that town, a Gallo-Roman furnace, having
its roof constructed with *Tegulæ* and *Imbrices*.   It is to be regretted that this
interesting monument was not better cared for.   It fell in ruins in 1873.

It happened one day when I was absent during the dinner hour of my workmen, that an English lady and her son came to see the diggings. The latter amused himself in working with a pick about that part of the construction in the room No. 1 which resembled a chimney, where he discovered a polished stone celt of a white colour, which he showed to his mother : neither of them, however, was aware of its value, and it was flung aside amongst the debris to be carted away. It was not until the following day, when I happened to show them the polished stone celts in the museum at Carnac, that they informed me of their discovery, and regretted that they had not known better. Exertions were made to recover the lost axe, but without success. This discovery of a stone axe in what appeared to be a chimney was all the more interesting from its correlation with a custom still observed at Carnac, that of building into the chimney of the dwelling-house a stone celt which is supposed to preserve the house from being struck by lightning. It is to be noted also that the name of the stone axe or celt in the Breton language is *Mein-Gurun*, that is to say, the Thunder Stone.

There were only a few objects in bronze found, viz.—

A buckle of a square form. (A, pl. III. fig. 1, natural size.)

A piece of wire or rod measuring 4 inches in length, and $\frac{1}{4}$ inch in breadth.

A ring of elliptic form, probably part of the buckle of a waist-belt. (A, pl. III. fig. 2, natural size.)

The head of a nail or button $1\frac{1}{4}$ inch in diameter, which may have been mounted either on leather garments, or on harness. The zingaris or gipsies of Hungary, and the Wallachians, to this day, employ similar buttons to adorn their

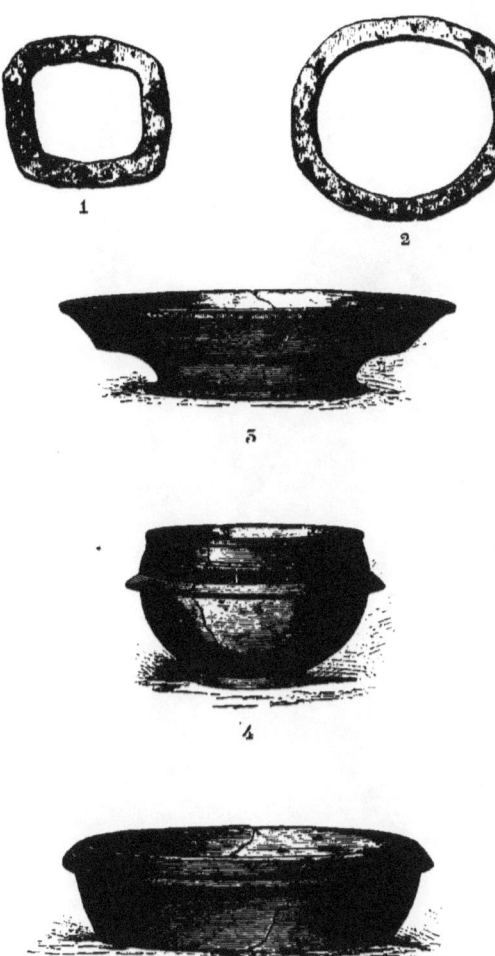

1

2

3

4

E.N.

5

A, PLATE III.

leather vestments, as may be seen by referring to the studies made by Valerio in Hungary and Wallachia. The Breton peasants, in many communes, still wear a number of metal buttons on their garments which are disposed more for ornament than use.

Lumps of iron and scoriæ were found in considerable quantity in the room No. 1, especially near the construction which has been indicated as resembling a forge. Several other pieces of iron, which appeared to have been parts of sword-blades and spear-heads, were also found on the floor, but they crumbled away after extraction and exposure to the air. The only objects in iron obtained entire were a few nails 2 to 3 inches in length. These were extracted from the east wall, where the lime mortar had preserved them.

Among the few fragments of glass found, some were portions of cups in white glass, while others of a bluish-green colour, ornamented with fluted mouldings, were evidently parts of square-shaped bottles similar to the Gallo-Roman bottles exhibited in the museums of Caen, Quimper, and Vannes. These fragments were found in the rooms Nos. 2, 3, and 4.

There were also found in these rooms some fragments of fine clear glass, very thin and pure, and a large piece of a bowl in fine clear glass, ornamented with two circular lines engraved not quite parallel.

A considerable quantity of bones and teeth of oxen of a small size were collected here. One of the bones had clean incisions on it, made by a sharp cutting implement; others bore the marks of the teeth of carnivora which had gnawed them. Several had been split lengthways, either to extract the marrow, or as the first step in the process of fabricating them into implements.

c

There were also found bones and teeth of the deer, goat, sheep, and pig. One tooth was found which belonged either to the dog or wolf.

In a locality so close to the sea, it was to be expected that the remains of edible molluscs would not be wanting, and so it proved, for there was an abundance of the shells of oysters, clams, *ormers*, limpets, and mussels. The oyster-shells were the most numerous. On comparing these with shells fresh from the Bay of Quiberon, no difference could be observed either in the enamel or in the dimensions.

Besides these, there was found in the trench cut on the outside of the east wall a veritable kitchen midden, composed of shells, bones, and fragments of pottery. This heap appeared to have been the refuse which had been thrown out of the dwelling.

The quantity of fragments of pottery collected during the excavation was very large in proportion to the small size of the dwelling, and thus denoted a certain amount of luxury. The whole of the fragments when collected together were sufficient to fill three baskets, which weighed 71 lbs. net.

I attempted, but without success, to reconstruct complete vases from these numerous fragments. It was with the greatest difficulty that two or three fragments were found which adapted themselves so as to be cemented together, and it became a puzzle to ascertain what had become of all the other fragments.

But the principal cause of astonishment was not so much the abundance of these fragments as the extreme diversity of the forms of the vases to which they belonged. This diversity of form, when taken in connection with their difference of texture and variety of ornament, indicates that they must have belonged to very different epochs.

A mere cursory inspection is in fact sufficient to show that some of these vases had been fashioned with neither taste nor art, and from rude materials collected from the surface of the ground; whilst others indicate, by the elegance of their forms and by the careful preparation of their material, that the makers had a considerable knowledge of the ceramic art.

A more careful examination of the fragments belonging to the first of these two categories enables one to perceive, from their irregularity of form and from their inequality of thickness, that they had been made by hand without the aid of the potter's wheel. The marks of the fingers are plainly visible on many of these fragments, whilst others bore a sort of ornament formed by the print of the potter's finger round the rim, and, judging from the smallness and shape of these, one would say that they had been made by women.*

Their paste is formed of earth, consisting of the debris of primitive rocks, and badly worked, in which one can easily distinguish, without the aid of a magnifying-glass, small fragments of quartz, felspar, mica, etc. The fracture is earthy, and the firing imperfect and unequal. They have in this respect a remarkable resemblance to the funeral vases found in the dolmens and kistvaens which are generally regarded as belonging to a very remote period.

It may be as well to add that in pointing out this striking similarity, I do not believe myself authorised to assign the rude pottery of the Bossenno to the remote epoch of the dolmens; but it appears to me to be shown by this comparison that the resemblance which exists between the

* At Rieux and at Malansac, which are villages inhabited by potters, situated in the Department of the Morbihan, it is the women who make all the pottery for ordinary use. The men make only the large vases called *pones* or *charniers*.

c 1

products of ages so far apart may become, in many cases, a
source of error, and that great caution must be exercised
when rude pottery is made the subject of a chronological
classification.

The following narrative is adduced in support of this
opinion :—

I happened to be in the Hebrides during the summer of
1868. The weather was tempestuous, and I had found a
shelter from a thunderstorm in the cottage of an old woman,
originally from the island of Tiree, but then living in Iona.
Two or three small vases that were placed on the table
attracted my attention. They were so like the ancient
pottery of the dolmens or kistvaens, that I asked where they
had been found. To my surprise the old woman replied, " I
did not find them, I made them myself."

" That must be impossible," I said, " for you have no
furnace to fire them."

" I do not need a furnace for that, and if you like I will
make you some."

" Do so by all means, I will be very glad to have two or
three of them."

The old woman went immediately out to her garden, and
brought back a quantity of argillaceous earth. She then
wetted the surface of the table, on which she moulded very
neatly, and in a short space of time, three small vases, which
bore the impress of her fingers round the outside of the neck,
and on the inside of the rim there was a border formed with
the points of her finger nails. She then said to me,

" I cannot proceed further just now, because the pots must
be dried before they are put on the fire. Come to-morrow
morning at ten o'clock, and you shall see that I do not require
a furnace to fire them."

At ten o'clock next morning I returned to the cottage. The only fireplace was a slab of stone in the centre of the room, on which a few pieces of turf were burning. The old woman placed the vases on the fire, poured milk into them, and allowed them to remain until the milk had boiled for some time. When this operation, which did not much exceed half-an-hour, was concluded, the vases had acquired sufficient hardness, and had all the appearance of the ancient pottery of the dolmens.

Returning to the description of the pottery of the Bossenno, several fragments of coarse gray pottery were found in the Mound A, which bore a more elaborate decoration than those described in the preceding pages. This decoration, which is by some authors designated geometric, consisted of a series of hollow black lines forming chevrons and lozenges. (See C, pl. XIII. figs. 5 and 6.) Several very fine specimens of vases of this kind, which had been found in excavations at Arradon and Carhaix, are exhibited in the museums of Vannes and Quimper. Several specimens similar to these are to be seen in the museum of the manufactory at Sevres. These had been found in Egypt, however, and they are figured and described by Brogniart,[1] as of the time of the Ptolemies, that is about the middle of the third century before the Christian era. Can this similarity of pottery found in Egypt and in Brittany be accounted for by the fact of African soldiers having been stationed in the Morbihan and in Finistère ? The *Notitia Dignitatum* of the Empire gives the principal military stations for the fourth century, and mentions *prefectus militum Maurorum* Venetorum Venetis, and again prefectus militum Maurorum Osismiacorum Osismiis.

* *Traité des arts Céramiques* par Alex. Brogniart. Tome premier, page 503. Paris, Bechet Seune ; 1854.

c 2

To the pottery described in the preceding pages there are to be added some fragments of a small vase, very thin, well fired, and having a fine hard sonorous paste. The outer surface was covered with a dark metallic-looking glaze, with red ornaments in relief. The Museum of St. Germain-en-Laye possesses several similar vases found in the Department of the Lozère. Three fragments of vases of the same kind are exhibited in the Guild Hall Museum, London, which

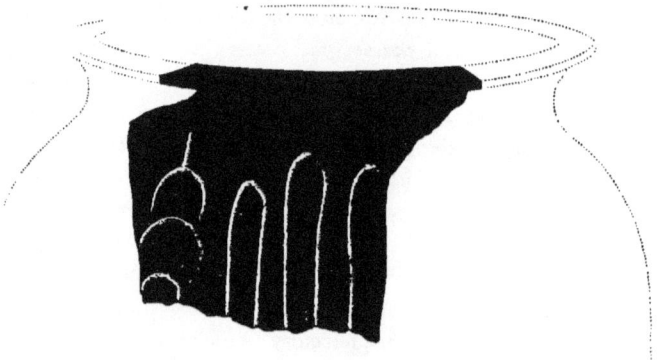

FRAGMENT OF POTTERY FOUND IN LONDON.

were found at a depth of 42 feet when the foundations of the Royal Exchange were sunk. In my subsequent excavations in the Mounds B and C, numerous fragments of this curious class of pottery were discovered, which enabled me to reconstruct the vase figured in the accompanying chromo-lithograph, A, pl. IV.

The greater portion of the pottery found in the Mound A was formed of common yellow, gray, and black earth, and consisted of fragments of diotæ, amphoræ, and ordinary domestic vessels. I succeeded in determining the forms of two flat dishes, in common gray earth, which resemble those

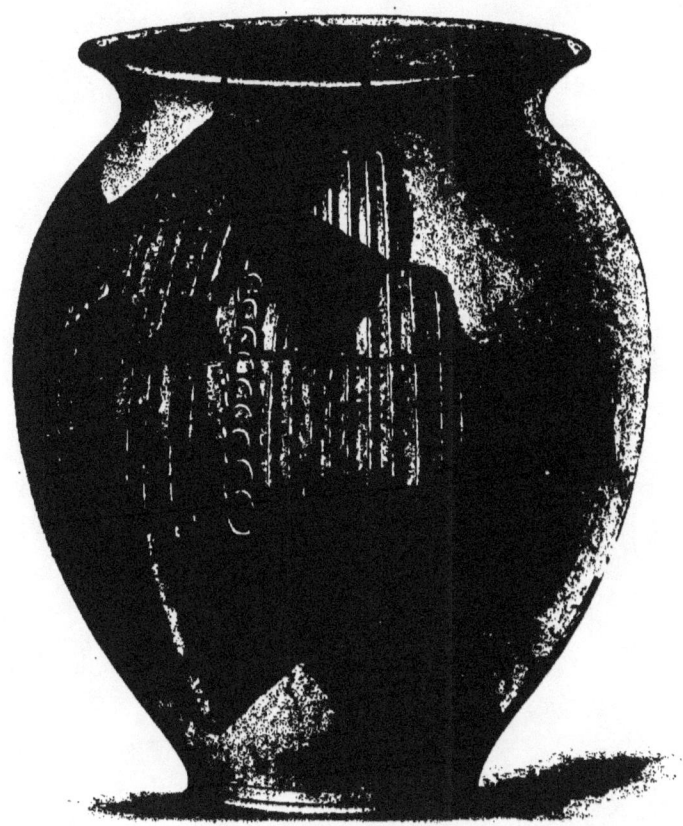

A, PLATE IV.
VASE FOUND IN MOUND C. (See p. 67.)

L. Cappé. Del.

Imp. Leroy &Pichon. Paris.

still in daily use at Carnac, called in the Breton dialect of Vannes, *er Cass*.   (See A, pl. III. fig. 5.)

Besides these fragments in gray, yellow, and black earth, the progress of the excavations brought to light some fragments in common red earth, and others, not so numerous, in the fine red earth, and with the lustrous glaze commonly called Samian.   From the latter fragments two small vases were reconstructed, one $5\frac{3}{4}$ and the other $3\frac{1}{2}$ inches in diameter (See A, pl. III., figs. 3 and 4.)   Some of these latter fragments appeared to me to belong to the class of pottery called " False Samian."   Birch describes this variety of pottery as covered with a thin red glazing due to a solution of sulphate of iron in which it had been plunged.   On trying to wash one of these fragments, so as to clear off the adhesive earth which covered it, the red glazing dissolved in the water, to which it imparted a bright red colour.   This experience showed the inexpediency of washing the fragments of pottery, even after they had been first carefully dried.

This enumeration of the different specimens of pottery found in the Mound A may now be concluded by mentioning a number of rods or stalks in coarse red earth, which were scattered about the floor of the room No. 1.   These measured 4 to 7 inches in length, and 1 to $1\frac{1}{2}$ inches in diameter.   It is believed by many antiquaries that these rods were made use of, in the places where pottery was made, to support the apodal vases and pieces with round bottoms during the firing,* and also for cleaning the hands of the potter, by rubbing, when too much empasted.

Lamps and coins are generally found in the diggings made

---

* To this day, in the Breton potteries, unvarnished vases are supported, whilst enamelled vases are isolated by little rods of refractory earth, having different forms, called *pernettes*.

in Gallo-Roman establishments, but no traces of either of these were found in the Mound A.

As soon as the diggings were completed the peasants commenced to clear away the ruins which had been exposed, as they wished to put the ground under pasture. In demolishing the east wall they discovered a small head of Venus in terra cotta, having an ornamant round the forehead formed of stars and small circles, with a point in their centre. As the neck bore the evidence of having been freshly broken, I caused a search to be made, in the hope of finding at least some other portion of the statuette, but without success.

The season was too far advanced to think of attacking another mound this year, and the diggings were therefore adjourned until the spring of 1875.

WINDOW AT BOURGEREL.

III.

EXCAVATIONS IN THE MOUND B.

Villa (?room).   *Cavroom.*   *Subterraneam.*

To face page 26.

B, PLATE I.—VIEW BETWEEN THE MOUNDS B AND C.

THE MOUND B.

THE results obtained from the excavation of the small mound, undertaken in the month of September 1874, were so far satisfactory as to lead me to look for still better results from the larger mounds, and in this I was not disappointed. As soon as the weather permitted, in the spring of 1875, the diggings were recommenced; and with a dozen of workmen, most of whom had been rendered more skilful by the experience of the previous year, an attack was made successively on the mounds marked in the plan of the Bossenno by the letters B and C. Although the work was commenced in reality on the Mound C, still it will render the description more clear to the reader if the diggings in the Mound B are first described, as the constructions found under the Mound C were only a dependence of the habitation found under the Mound B.

The Mound B measured from north to south 82 feet in length, and had a breadth of 56 feet. Its average height was about 7 feet. An excavation on its summit indicated that some one had already been at work there. My workmen, who belonged to the locality, stated that there was a tradition to that effect in the country.

The example of my predecessors was not followed in our commencing operations on the summit, but on the north side, where we soon struck on a wall, at the base of which was a square space 5 feet 11 inches of a side, paved with Roman roofing tiles, or *Tegulæ*. These tiles had their crotchet edges turned downwards, and were solidly imbedded in cement, so as to form a smooth piece of pavement.[*]

The wall was followed all round the mound until the exterior of the building was entirely exposed to view, after which the clearing out of the interior was proceeded with.

When the latter operation was concluded, we had exposed to view a building of rectangular form, measuring 62 feet in length by 47 feet in breadth, and composed of eleven subdivisions—viz., three large apartments and a passage, Nos. 2, 3, 4, and 10 of the ground-plan. These occupied the centre of the building. On the east side there were the room No. 11, and the corridor No. 1. On the west side there was a suite of small rooms, Nos. 5, 6, 7, 8, 9, probably *cubicula*. The dilapidated state of the exterior wall on the west side prevented our ascertaining if there had been any entrances on this side. The principal entrance of the building is indicated on the ground-plan.

The thickness of the exterior walls was 24 inches, and that of the interior 20 inches.

The west wall was prolonged to the north to where it joined on to the building found under the Mound C (the baths). A court, which measured 27 feet in breadth, separated the two buildings.

These indications being sufficient to give a general idea of the form, character, and relations of the two buildings, we now proceed to give a more detailed description of each of the eleven subdivisions of the larger structure, all of which

---

[*] See the ground-plan B, pl. II.

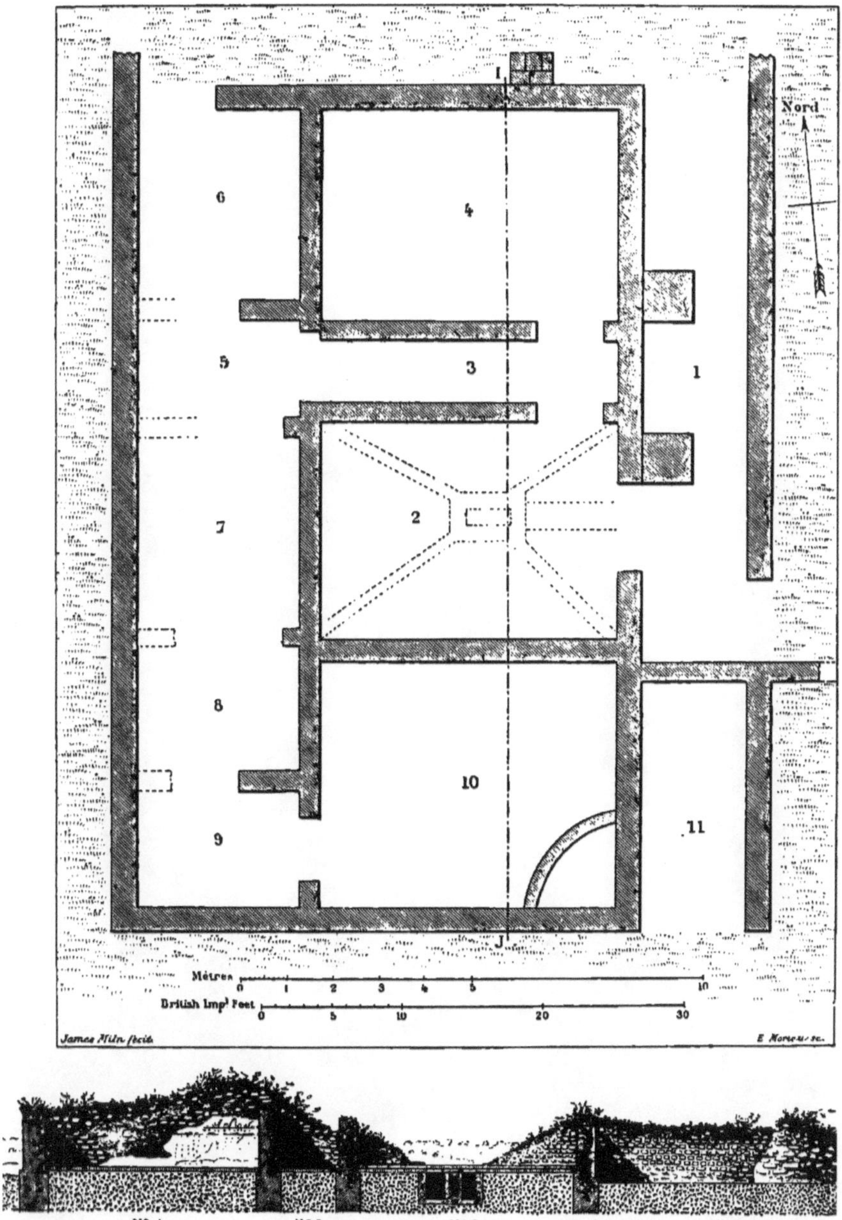

Nord

6
4
5
3
1
7
2
8
10
9
11

Métres

British Imp? Feet

0   1   2   3   4   5   10

0   5   10   20   30

James Miln fecit.   E Morieu sc.

Nº 4   Nº 3   Nº 2   Nº 10

II, PLATE II.—PLAN AND SECTION OF THE BUILDING IN THE MOUND B.

bore marks of having been destroyed by fire. Their relative positions and dimensions will be more readily understood by reference to the ground-plan of the Mound B.

No. 1.   A passage 42 feet in length, by 7 feet 6 inches in breadth.   The height of what remained of the walls was on the south side 6 feet, on the east 1 foot 3 inches, on the west 6 feet 6 inches.

This passage had a doorway on the east side, which appears to have been the principal entrance to the building; whilst on the north it opened on the court already mentioned as situated between the buildings B and C.*   The east wall seemed to be continued until it joined on to the baths under the Mound C; but this could not be verified, as the tenant of the grazing objected to the diggings being carried on in the little bit of pasture between the Mounds B and C.

Two square buttresses measuring 1 foot 4 inches on each side supported the west wall of the passage.   One of these buttresses was not bonded into the wall.   This seemed to indicate that it had been added to the building after its construction.

An opening to the south of these buttresses led into the interior of the building by a small staircase which ascended from the passage to the room No. 2.   This staircase was in a very dilapidated condition, and fell to pieces during the excavation.   Underneath it were found the traces of a furnace, with a very small aperture, which had served to heat the hypocaust under the room No. 2.

The few courses of masonry that remained of the east wall of the passage were in a very dilapidated condition.

* See the plan of the Bossenno.

No. 2. This room measured 21 feet in length by 16 in breadth. The height of what remained of the walls was

		ft.	in.
On the north side		3	4
„ south	„	2	8
„ east	„	2	5
„ west	„	2	10

This room appeared to have been the principal chamber of the mansion, and had two entrances; the one from the staircase above mentioned, the other from another passage, No. 3. It was built upon a hypocaust of a very remarkable construction. The ground-plan shows the direction of the conduits which served to circulate the heated air under the floor of the apartment. These were built with undressed stones without mortar, and formed a sort of St. Andrew's cross, in the axis of which was a pillar, of similar construction, measuring 2 feet 8 inches in length by 11 inches in breadth. They were covered with large slabs of granite, except at the eastern extremity of the pillar, where a large brick tile, measuring 3 feet square and 3 inches thick, and pierced with a round hole at one of its corners, had been substituted. Two layers of cement 6 inches thick formed the floor of the room, and covered the hypocaust.

The walls, and also the covering slabs of the conduits, were still black from smoke, whilst the interior was one-third full of soot and charcoal. This circumstance leaves no doubt as to the use of these conduits. They had evidently been constructed for the purpose of heating the apartment, and not to act as drains. In the Gallo-Roman villa discovered at Mané-Bourgerel, in the Morbihan, a similar hypocaust was

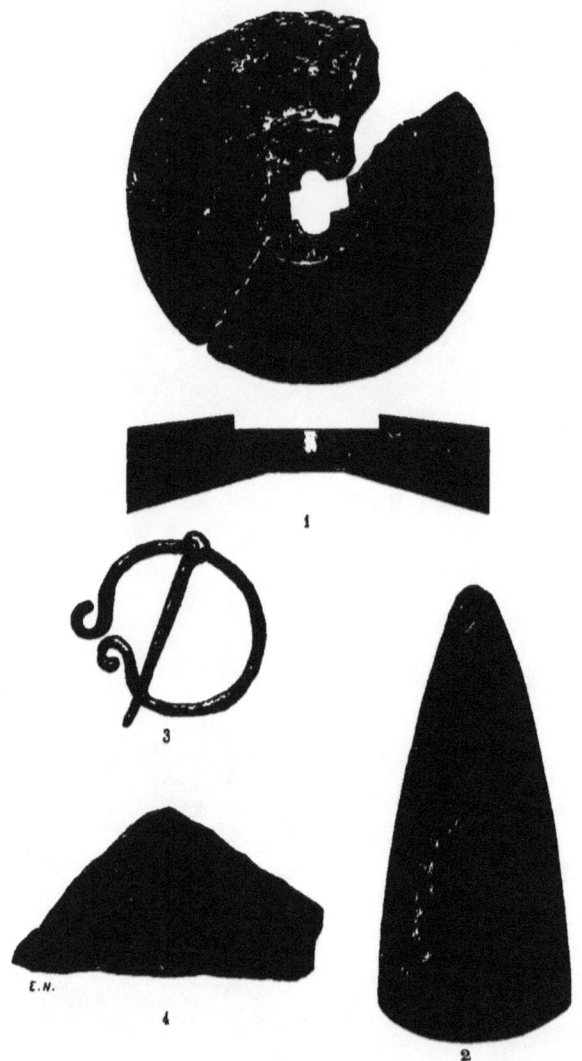

1

3

2

E.N.

4

B, PLATE III.

found, of which De Caumont gives the plan in his *Ere gallo-romaine.*[*]

On lifting the covering slabs at the corners of the apartment, we were surprised to find on the ends of the conduits the following objects, which appeared to have been placed there intentionally :—

1. At the north-east corner the broken fragments of a quern or hand-mill in granite, 16 inches in diameter, and reddened by the action of fire.   The granite of Carnac takes this tint after being burnt.   (B, pl. III. fig. 1, bis, reduced.)

2. At the south-east angle a polished celt in diorite, 5½ inches long, and beside it some fragments of blue glass, and of the red lustrous ware called Samian.   (B, pl. III. fig. 2.)

3. At the north-west corner fragments of common pottery in gray and black earth.

4. At the south-west corner a small opaque bead of a turquoise-blue colour.   Several similar beads, which had apparently formed parts of a necklace, were afterwards found in the progress of the diggings.

These objects, it may be repeated, appeared to have been placed intentionally in the places where they were discovered, and possibly in conformity with some superstition which is

* " Villa de Mané-Bourgerel (Morbihan).—Je dois à M. Jaquemet, ingénieur en chef des ponts et chaussées, le plan d'un autre *villa* découverte à Mané-Bourgerel, mais on n'a reconnu qu'une partie des fondations ; il en reste d'autres dans les pièces voisines, de sorte que je me borne à présenter (p. 392) le plan qu'à bien voulu me communiquer M. Jaquemet, sans essayer d'indiquer la destination des appartements.   La pièce J était remarquable par un hypocauste d'une forme particulière.   Le plan montre la direction de conduits qui faisaient circuler la chaleur sous le sol ; j'ai vu à Vieux un hypocauste semblable dont les conduits étaient en partie creusés dans la roche calcaire au-dessous du pavé, ce qui prouve que les moyens les plus simples étaient quelquefois employés."—*Ere gallo-romaine*, 2ᵉ édit., p. 390.

now unknown. In support of this statement, the reader is referred to the description given in the account of the excavations of the Mound A (page 16), of a very ancient custom still existing in Brittany, viz. that of placing a polished stone celt in the chimney to preserve the house against lightning.

As fewer roofing tiles were found when clearing out the room No. 2 than in the other apartments, it was supposed that it might have been the *atrium* of the dwelling, but after the discovery of the hypocaust this hypothesis became less admissible.

No. 3 was a passage communicating with the vestibule No. 5, and with the apartments Nos. 2 and 4. It measured 22 feet 6 inches in length and 4 feet 6 inches in breadth.

A red band, two inches broad, had been painted along the plaster which covered the walls at a height of 2 feet 5 inches from the floor. Other remains of mural decoration were found in the bottom of the passage, but in such a bad state of preservation that the design could not be fully made out.

No. 4.—One of the principal rooms of the house measured 21 feet in length and 16 feet in breadth. The entrance to it was from the passage just described.

The average height of the walls was on the north side 3 feet; on the south 3 feet 10 inches; on the east 5 feet; and on the west 4 feet.

The walls of this room had been covered with three coats of plaster, each half-an-inch in thickness. Traces of mural decoration in red, yellow, dark gray, and blue, were visible on the second coat of plaster, and a series of small holes had been picked in it, evidently for the purpose of making the third coat of plaster adhere. This also bore traces of having been

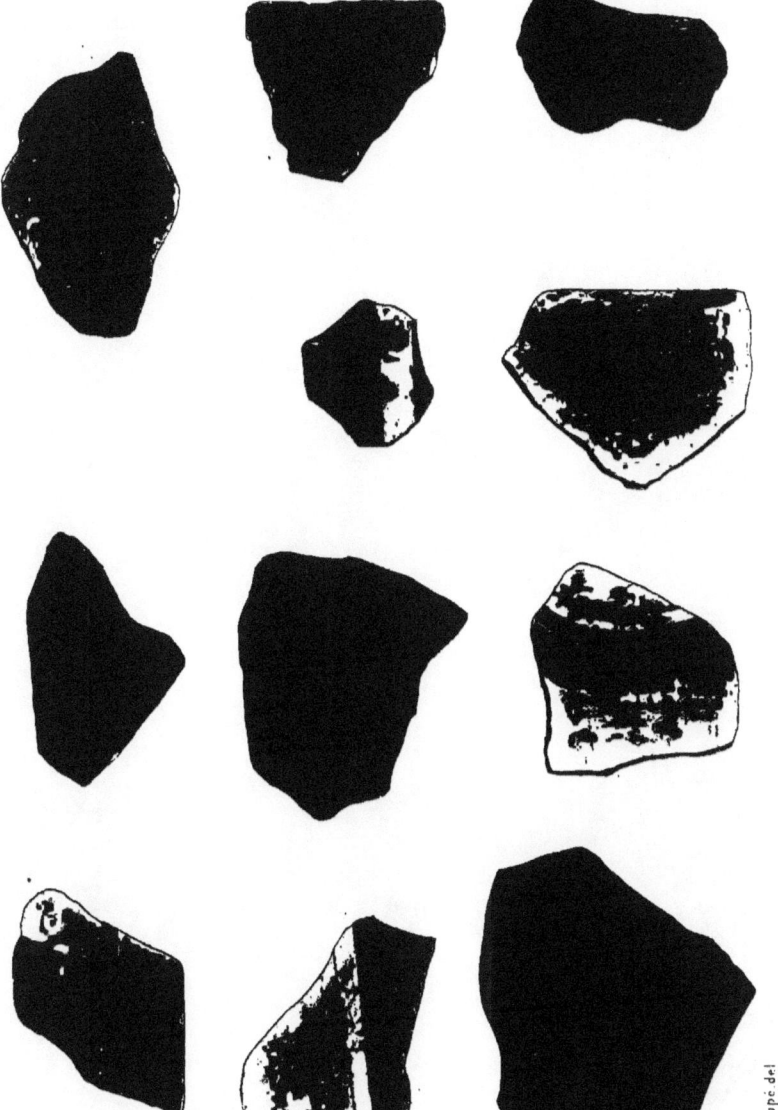

L. Cappé del

To face page 3.

B, PLATE IV.—FRAGMENTS OF PAINTED WALL PLASTER (Reduced).

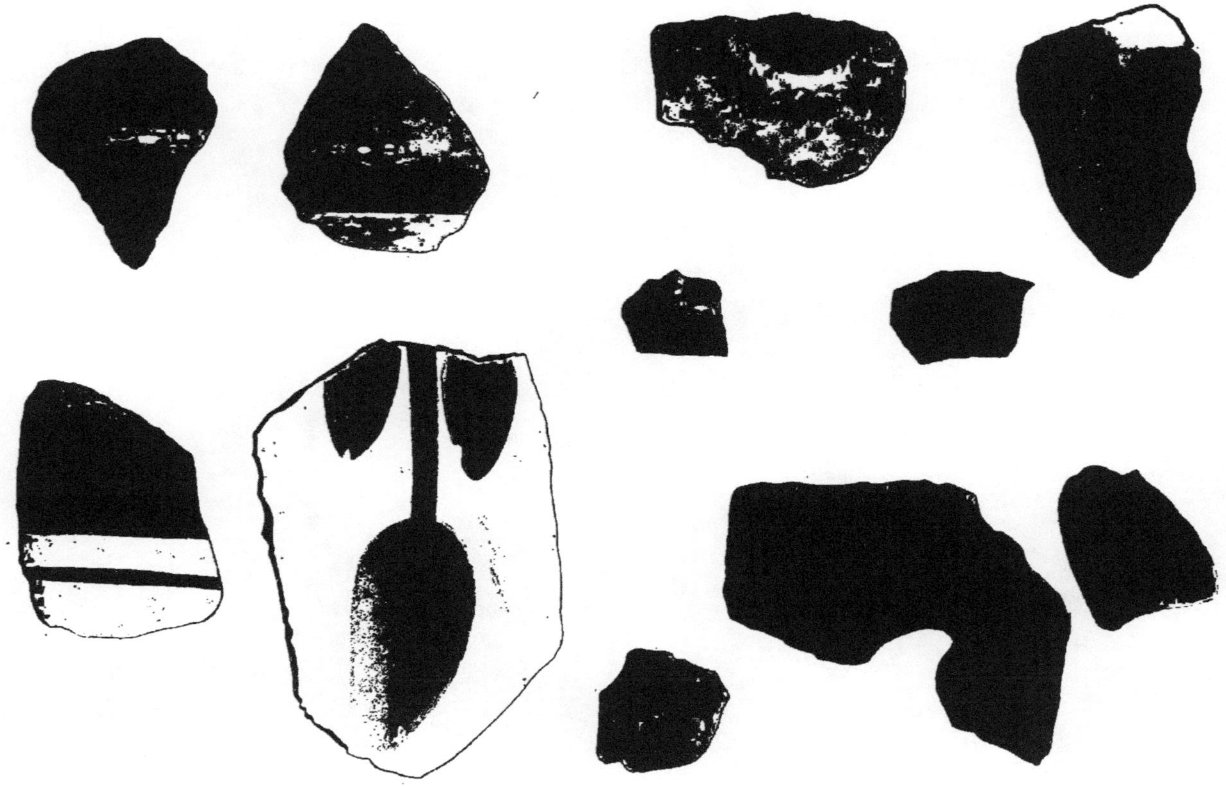

painted in similar colours, but of a different design. (See the section of the Mound B, pl. II.) An attempt to find out the complete design of the decoration of this chamber failed from the want of sufficient data, and owing to the small number and diminutive size of the painted fragments of plaster which remained adhering to the walls.

No. 5.—This little room, situated at one end of the passage No. 3, appeared to have been a vestibule, and measured 12 feet in length by 7 feet in breadth. It would seem probable that there must have been an opening here for communicating with the exterior, but this hypothesis could not be verified, as only the foundations of the west wall remained.

Nos. 6, 7, 8.—These three little rooms appeared to have been the sleeping apartments, *cubicula*, of the mansion.

The first of these, No. 6, measured 14 feet in length by 11 feet 6 inches in breadth, and communicated by a doorway with No. 5. Although the north wall was in a very dilapidated condition, one could still make out the remains of a doorway which opened on the court, situated between the Mound B and the Mound C (the baths).

The second bedroom, No. 7, measured 14 feet in length by 11 feet 6 inches in breadth.

The third bedroom, No. 8, measured 9 feet in length, and 10 feet 6 inches in breadth, and communicated with the rooms No. 7 on the north and No. 9 on the south.

Following the same method of working as in the Mound A, trenches were cut under the floors of these bedrooms to a depth of 4 feet. At that depth we found traces of an anterior building and diverse objects, amongst which were a circular

D

bronze brooch of Celtic type with short pin (B, pl. III. fig. 3, natural size) ; fragments of a cup in white glass, and of square formed bottles in blue glass ; several iron objects very much oxidised, which seemed to have been the fastenings of doors ; also numerous fragments of pottery, in gray and black earth, of simple forms, and with straight rims.

No. 9.—This little room, measuring 8 feet 6 inches by 11 feet 6 inches, communicated with the rooms No. 8 on the north and No. 10 on the east side.

The partition walls between these five rooms, Nos. 5, 6, 7, 8, 9, were very faintly indicated on the floor, and were difficult to make out.

No. 10.—This room measured 21 feet in length by 18 feet in breadth. The mean height of the walls was on the north 4 feet ; on the south 3 feet 10 inches ; on the east 5 feet 5 inches ; and on the west side 5 feet 5 inches.

It communicated by a doorway with No. 9. The floor was 12 inches below the level of the other apartments.

A curious construction was discovered in the south-east corner, shaped like a beehive or baker's oven, and roughly built of large stones of irregular shape. Between it and the north wall of the apartment there was found a layer of large round stones, cemented into the floor. I caused a hole to be dug inside this beehive-like structure to a depth of 6 feet below the level of the floor, but the excavation yielded nothing save the neck of a bottle in blue glass. This curiously shaped structure may possibly have been an oven or furnace, and this conjecture is strengthened by the fact of an opening having been discovered in the wall of No. 11 choked up with rubbish which might have answered for the mouth of the furnace.

The large quantity of bones, shells of edible molluscs, and fragments of domestic pottery, found in the room No. 10, leave but little doubt as to its destination. It had been the kitchen.

Besides the bones and shells there were also found in this room several round discs in brick earth, and some weights in polished granite, which may probably have been used as sinkers for nets.

At this date the sea does not come within a mile of the Bosseno, but formerly it had come close to it. The proprietor, M. le Guennec of Kerfraval, showed me one of his titles of that holding, dated 1740, which proves that in the last century the sea came up to the lower fields of the Bossenno. This title makes mention of a number of pieces of land, one of which is therein described as

" Une piece de terre sous pature *Ker-guin-goh*, au mette (*sic*) de laquelle est une source d'eau, et une pièce de terre sous pature et jonc qui se couvre de mer aux grands eaux," etc.*

No. 11.—This room measured 18 feet in length by 7 feet 6 inches in breadth.

The average height of the walls was, on the north 5 feet 10 inches ; on the east 3 feet ; and on the west side 3 feet 8 inches.

This room seemed to have been made use of as an annexe to the kitchen, and for attending to the furnace above mentioned. As no traces of even the foundations of a stone wall

---

* Description et declaration par mesurage et debornement, fait en l'etude de M. Henry, notaire royal registrateur, controlée à Auray le 24 decembre 1740, à titre de domaine congéable.

could be found, it must be supposed that it had been closed at
the south end by a barrier or wooden partition.

This mansion, of which we conclude a detailed description by that of the room No. 11, had been very carefully built
of small cubic stones of equal sizes, the courses of which were
regulated, at regular intervals, by layers of tiles. The floors
of all the apartments were formed of thick layers of cement,
and the walls were covered with coats of plaster, excepting
the room No. 6, which had none.

The site had been fitly chosen, as well from its convenience
as for the pleasing view it commanded of the surrounding
country. The Mont Saint Michel had sheltered it against
the west winds which came off the Bay of Biscay—to this day
the most violent in Brittany. Numerous springs of good
water still exist all round the Bossenno. The field numbered
665 in the map of the Bossenno bears the name *Er goh fetan
tal parc piard* (the old fountain near the stony field). Another
fountain (which is said never to fail) is situated in a field
farther to the east, and is named *Fetan ker in goh* (the
fountain of the old town). The means of communication
may possibly have been by the old road leading from Carnac
to the Trinité-sur-mer, which still traverses the Bossenno.
Tradition points it out as having been a road before the
Roman occupation.

The following enumeration contains the description of the
different objects found in each of the rooms of this dwelling:—

Iron nails of different sizes, and numerous fragments of
Gallo-Roman pottery of many different kinds were found in
all the rooms. With the view of avoiding repetition, the more
noteworthy objects only will be indicated in the order of the
numbers of the apartments.

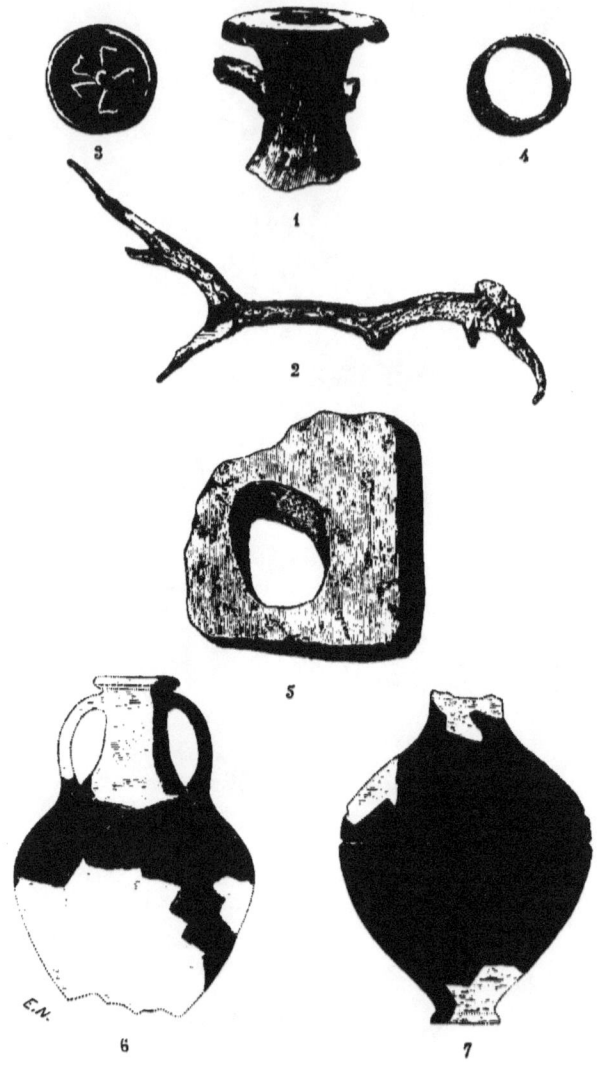

B, PLATE VI.

In the passage No. 1 were found many fragments of curious pottery in fine paste, hard and sonorous, ornamented in relief with diagonal bands and chains. From these fragments several vases were reconstructed, similar to that figured in the chromo-lithograph A, pl. IV.

Part of the neck of an amphora, 3½ inches in length, in red earth, and having two handles, was also found here. (B, pl. VI. fig. 1.)

In the room No. 2, one of the antlers of a deer (*Cervus elaphus*), 2 feet 8 inches in length, was discovered near the doorway communicating with the passage No. 3. (B, pl. VI. fig. 2.)

Near the antler was the head of a small brooch in bronze (B, pl. VI. fig. 3, natural size), also an engraved ring in bronze (B, pl. VI. fig. 4, natural size), and a small brass of Claudius II., on which :—

DIVO CLAVDIO.   Head radiated and turned to the right.

Reverse : CONSECRATIO.   An eagle erect and turning to the left.   This coin had been struck after the death of the Emperor Claudius.   (Cohen, 49.)

Several pieces of iron very much oxidised were scattered about the floor, and seemed to be parts of sword-blades.

Two objects in stone were also found here.   The one was a polisher in gray schist, similar to that found in the Mound A.   The other was a portion of a painter's palette in a fine white stone, measuring 3 inches in length, by 3 inches in breadth.   (B, pl. VI. fig. 5.)

With the different fragments of pottery collected in this room I succeeded in reconstructing

A lagena, diameter 7 inches, in yellow earth, having two handles and a straight neck, with a bourrelet or collar in relief.   (B, pl. VI. fig. 6.)

A pear-shaped lagena, diameter 7½ inches, in yellow earth, without handles, having two parallel bands engraved, the neck wanting. (B, pl. VI. fig. 7.)

A terrine, diameter 10½ inches, in gray earth, with a bourrelet or collar in relief on the outer rim, and having a spout. (B, pl. VII. fig. 1.)

A vase of ovoid shape, height 9½ inches, diameter 8½ inches, in coarse grayish brown earth, having a large mouth, with a circular rim projecting outwards, and twelve horizontal bands painted black superposed. (B, pl. VII. fig. 2.)

In the passage No. 3 the upper and lower stones of a quern or hand-mill, in lava, 14 inches in diameter, were found on the floor opposite the doorway of the room No. 43, and also several fragments of red lustrous ware, two specimens of which are figured, viz.—

1. Fragment of a bowl with ornaments divided in compartments in relief. In one compartment a winged figure, in the other a boar's head. (B, pl. VII. fig. 3, reduced one half.)

2. Fragment of the same kind ornamented with a circular band of vertical lines, stamped hollow. (B, pl. VII. fig. 4, reduced one half.)

In the room No. 4 :

Fragment of a deer's horn having cuts made by a sharp instrument on its base.

A bodkin or stylus in polished bone, similar to one which was afterwards found in the room No. 10. (B, pl. VIII. fig. 4.)

A bead of a turquoise-blue colour, opaque, ¾ of an inch in diameter, probably part of a necklace.

A small brass of Tetricus the younger :—

CAIVS PIVS. ESV. TETRICVS. CAES. (Caius

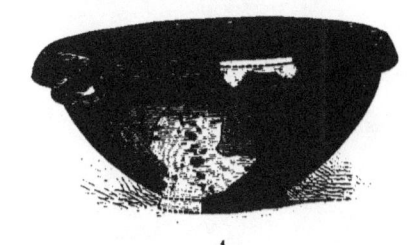

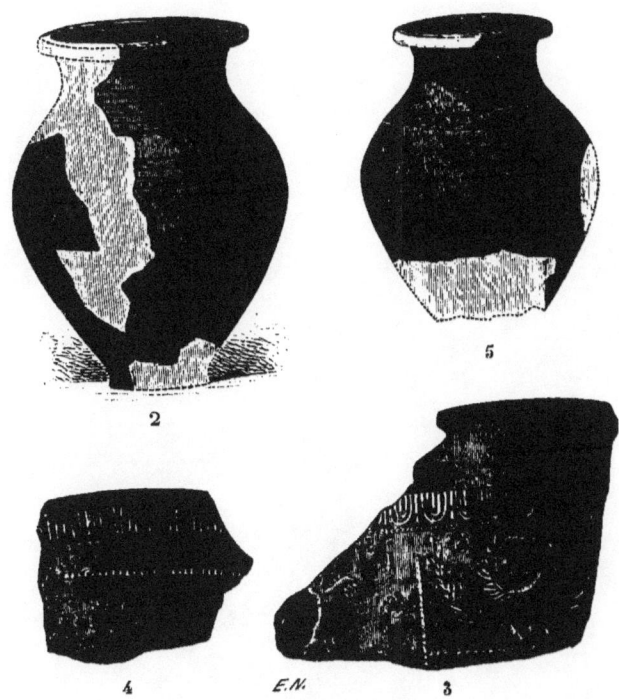

B, PLATE VII.

Pius Esuvius Tetricus Cæsar). His head radiated, turned to the right, and having the paludamentum.

Reverse defaced.

A second brass of Gallienus :—

GALLIENVS. AVG. (Gallienus Augustus); head turned to the right.

Reverse: LIBERO. P. CONS. AVG. (Libero patri conservatori Augusti.) Panther passing to the left. On the exergue B. (Cohen, 337.)

A small brass of Constantine I.—

CONSTANS. NOB. CAES. (Constantius nobilis Cæsar.) The bust turned to the right, with the paludamentum.

Reverse: GLORIA EXERCITVS. Two soldiers helmeted, erect, facing each other, each holding a spear reversed and leaning on a shield; between them a staff surmounted by a flag. (Cohen, 131.)

The following vases were reconstructed from the various fragments of pottery found in this room :—

A vase in brownish-gray earth, of ovoid form, having a large mouth, the rim projecting outwards; on the shoulder three parallel lines coarsely engraved, and between two of these a line of hollow points; diameter $6\frac{3}{4}$ inches. (B, pl. VII. fig. 5.)

A vase of the same form, in bluish-gray earth, very large mouth, ornamented all round with hollow vertical lines in juxtaposition, separated at the shoulder by three hollow horizontal lines painted black; paste fine and well fired; diameter $6\frac{1}{2}$ inches. (B, pl. VIII. fig. 1.)

A bowl in grayish-brown earth, having a narrow base; diameter 7 inches. This form of bowl is still in use in some parts of Brittany. (B, pl. VIII. fig. 2.)

Three other fragments of pottery ought to be mentioned.

Part of the handle of a vase ; ornament formed by twisting. (B, pl. VIII. fig. 3.)

Fragment of a vase decorated with undulating lines. (B, pl. VIII. fig. 4.)

Fragment, in red earth, of the neck of a vase having the same ornament ; length 4½ inches.   (B, pl. VIII. fig. 5.)

The persistence of an ornamentation similar to that on the two fragments just described is very remarkable, and may perhaps be sufficient excuse for the following digression :—

Many nations have made use of these undulating lines as the symbol of running water.

We find it in the eleventh sign of the Zodiac ♒ *Aquarius*.

The ancient form of the Chinese character for water was similar to the eleventh sign of the Zodiac, and the symbol for distress consisted of the same sign with a bar across, ♒ picturing the stoppage of the irrigation in the rice-field.

It is also found in the symbols employed by the Egyptians to represent water 𓂝𓏭𓈖 mai 𓃾𓏭𓈖 mou. This symbol conveyed the idea of freshness or flowing. On the summit of funeral monuments it seemed to symbolise the flowing of time.[*]

The persistence of this ornamentation in the Morbihan from the most ancient times up to the present is to be remarked under very many conditions. It is found not only on the drinking cup in the funeral pottery of the dolmens, but also on the monoliths which form the supports of these monuments. One is tempted to compare these with the rendering of the Egyptian symbol just alluded to.

[*] See the *Dictionnaire d'Archéologie Égyptienne*, par Paul Pierret. Paris, Rollin and Feuardent, 1875.

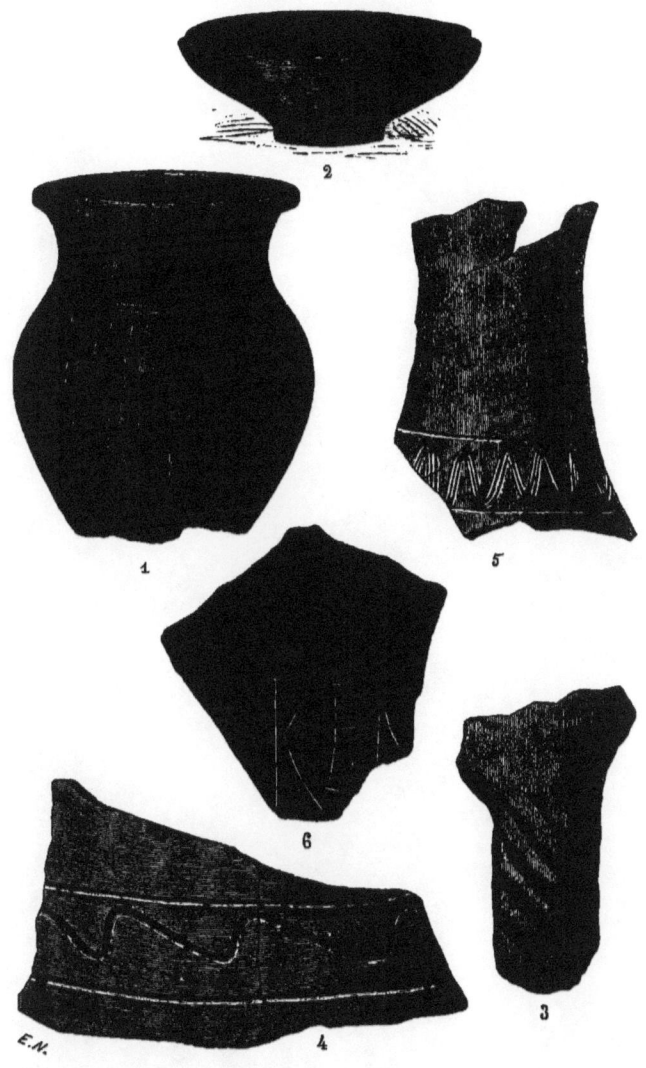

2

1

5

6

3

4

E.N.

To face page 40.

B. PLATE VIII.

These undulating lines are to be found on nearly all the Breton pottery of the last two centuries. They are to this day one of the most common forms of ornament used by the potters of Malansac, who fabricate without a wheel, that is by hand, by the method of procedure called *colombin*, large vases called charniers or pones.[*]

PONE OF MALANSAC.

The above engraving represents one of these pones which I drew in the workshop of a potter at Malansac.[†]

Whilst I was drawing this pone I asked the potter if he knew the meaning of these ornaments, and why he applied them. He replied to me, " I know several sorts of ornaments

[*] Vases 3 feet 6 inches in height, used for washing purposes, on which this design is applied in relief. For the manner in which these vases are made, see the *Traité des Arts Ceramiques*, par Alex. Brongniart, Tome i. page 391.

[†] This pone had another ornament, which is shown in the engraving, placed above the undulating lines. This sign is identically the same with one of the signs of the dolmens, classed by M. de Closmadeuc as the jugiform sign. There is in this fact another proof to add to so many others of the persistence of customs and traditions in Brittany.—See also *Sculptures Lapidaires et Signes gravés des Dolmens.* Vannes, 1873.

which we apply to different vases because we have always
done so, but as to their signification I know nothing, and I
never heard it spoken of."

This ornamentation of undulating lines is also to be seen
engraved on the arches over the doors of houses* (see the
drawing, page 50), and on the tombstones in the cemeteries,
ancient and modern, in the same department.

We now return to the description of the objects found in
the rooms of the building in Mound B.

In the room No. 5 nothing of any importance was found.

In the room No. 6 :
A second brass of Victorinus :—
IMP. C. VICTORINVS. P. F. AVG.   (Imperator
Cæsar Victorinus Pius Felix Augustus.)   The bust radiated,
turned to the right, with the paludamentum.
Reverse: PROVIDENTIA. AVG. (providentia Augusti).
Figure of Providence erect to the left, holding a rod and horn
of plenty ; at the feet a globe.   (Cohen, 57.)
Two small implements in yellow flint polished.   The
cutting face of one of these is notched from having been used.
A blue bead like turquoise, $\frac{1}{2}$ inch in diameter.
A flat dish in gray earth, 8 inches diameter, reconstructed
from fragments, and of the same description as the one
figured A, pl. III. fig. 5.

In the room No. 7 :
A small brass of Tetricus senior :—

* I owe this drawing to the kindness of Mr. Huray, architect. The
curious curve of the arch, reproduced mathematically, merits attention.

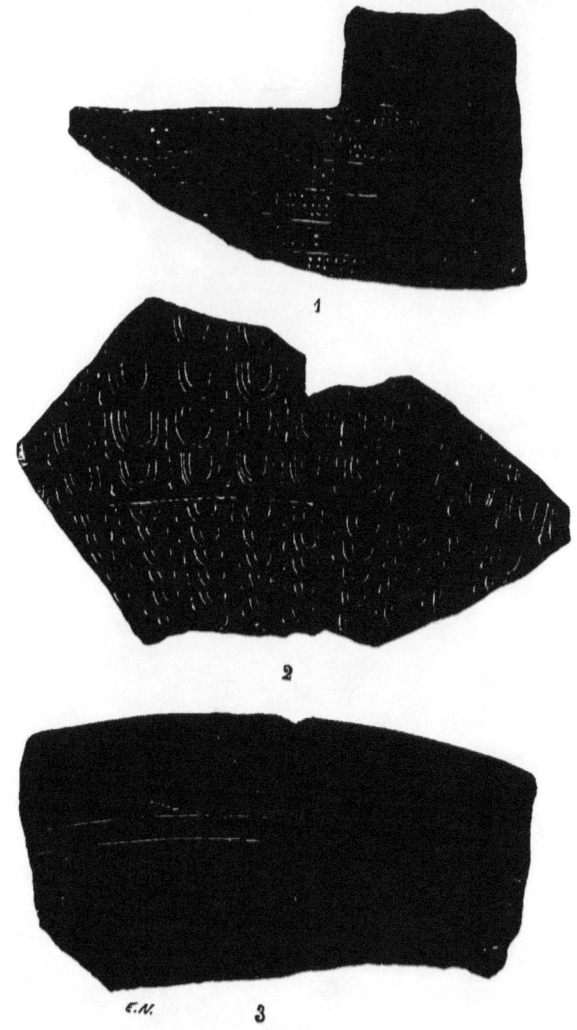

1

2

E.N.

3

B, PLATE IX.

CAIVS. PIVS. ESVVIVS. TETRICVS.

Reverse defaced.

Several pieces of marble pavement, white streaked with red.

A stone implement of a yellowish colour, polished by use, 2 inches in length, of the same kind as that figured A, pl. II. fig. 3.

Several dressed mouldings, in a fine white calcareous stone not found in the Morbihan. Several other dressed stones of the same nature were here found, which seemed to have formed parts of pillars, and which bore the traces of a thin coating of cement.

The archway of a door, constructed of white stones, cement, and bricks, placed alternately, lay upon the floor in the middle of the room. These stones, the quoins for the arch, bore the marks of the saw with which they had been cut from the block.

Fragment of a bowl in fine black earth, slightly glazed, having two letters complete, and a portion of a third skilfully engraved after the firing. (B, pl. VIII. fig. 6, natural size.)

In the room No. 8 :

Fragment of a vase in fine red lustrous ware, ornamented with zones of small rectangular figures in juxtaposition. Within these was another form of decoration, consisting of oblique lines and points in relief, obtained by pressure in moulds. (B, pl. IX. fig. 1, natural size.)

Fragment of the same nature, ornamented with zones of concentric ovolos or festoonings, also obtained by moulding. (B, pl. IX. fig. 2, natural size.)

In the room No. 9 :

A granite pestle, 5½ inches in length, of the same kind as that figured E, pl. II. fig. 1.

A small hemisphere in bronze, one inch in diameter, probably part of a button or ornament for harness.

Several boars' tusks.

A large quantity of bones of ruminants and shells of edible molluscs, especially of oysters. On submitting the latter to the inspection of Dr. du Gressy, who has contributed so largely to the advancement of oyster-culture in the Department of the Morbihan, he at once pronounced them to be of the same kind as the oysters of Quiberon.

There were also found here a great many fragments of pottery of different kinds.

Rounded discs of tile from 2 to 4 inches in diameter.

A bottle, reconstructed, in dark yellow earth, turbiniform, with narrow neck and base, and furnished with a handle inserted in the neck below a circular band in relief, ornamented with painted dark brown horizontal lines. Over all the vase, from the base of the neck downwards, there are horizontal dark brown bands in relief. Its height is 8 inches, diameter 6½ inches. (B, pl. X. fig. 1.)

Numerous fragments of coarse pottery of a Celtic type were collected in this little room. Of these the following specimens represent the most noteworthy.

Fragment of the rim of a bowl in brownish-black earth, badly fired, decorated with horizontal lines in relief; below these a series of hollow grain markings obtained by stamping. (B, pl. IX. fig. 3, natural size.)

Fragment of the same kind having a large band of undulating lines finely cut. (B, pl. X. fig. 2, natural size.)

1

2

4

E.N.   5

3

Fragment of the same kind decorated with circular lines in relief, having hollow grain markings rudely cut. (B, pl. X. fig. 5, natural size.)

Fragment of the same nature decorated with five horizontal bands of hollow grain markings. The middle band is composed of larger elongated hollows of an oval form irregularly and rudely cut by hand. Below these bands an indication of fern-leaf ornamentation similarly formed by hand. (B, pl. X. fig. 4, natural size.)

Fragment of the same sort adorned with hollow horizontal lines ; between two of these lines a large band of hollow grain markings similar to those in the preceding fragments, but arranged obliquely in three rows. (B, pl. X. fig. 3, natural size.)

Fragment of the rim of a bowl in dark gray earth having a letter or sign (?) engraved after the firing. (B, pl. XI. fig. 1, natural size.)

Fragment of a vase decorated with geometric figures of different kinds stamped hollow ; paste bluish gray, well fired. (B, pl. XI. fig. 2, natural size.)

Fragment of the handle of the same vase. (B, pl. XI. fig. 3, natural size.)

In clearing out the room No. 10, a large quantity of bones of ruminants and other animals, also numerous shells of edible molluscs, were found, as in the room No. 9.

Besides these there was also found a small brass attributed to Constantine the Great or his sons :—

VRBS ROMA.   Bust of Roma turned to the left, with the imperial mantle and helmet, an aigrette on the helmet.

Reverse without legend.   The wolf turned to the left,

suckling Romulus and Remus, and looking at them.   Above
these two stars.

A bodkin 6 inches in length, in polished bone. (B, pl. XI.
fig. 4.)

The vertebra of a young whale 5 inches in diameter,
having the edges rudely cut, so as to make it serviceable for a
pedestal or support.   (B, pl. XI. fig. 5.)

The half of a whistle or hunting call in bone, polished. (B,
pl. XI. fig. 6.)   This call is similar to some of those found
in the forest of Brotonne * now exhibited in the Museum of
Caen in Normandy, where the following drawing was made.
(B, pl. XI. fig. 7.)

A round stone, polished, in nephrite, called "œuf de
serpent," similar to those found in the Gallo-Roman cemetery
at Saint Jacques de Lisieux, and at Saint Symphorien, near
Vannes.

Two stones of ovoid form, in polished granite, having a
groove cut all round in their longer axis.   The larger of

---

* " Les os chez les Romains étaient employés, comme chez nous, à la
confection d'un grand nombre de petits ustensiles, tels que des cuillères, des
épingles à cheveux, des poinçons, des dés, etc.   On sait qu'on en fabriquait
aussi des flûtes.   Le nom latin *tibia* est dû à cette origine."

No. 312. " Fragment de flûte long de 10 centimètres, percé de deux trous.
Tronçon percé d'un seul trou circulaire à usage de sifflet.   Ces deux objects
proviennent des fouilles de Jort en 1852."

No. 313. " Deux tronçons semblables au précédent, dont la longueur
n'excède pas 25 millimètres, provenant des fouilles de la forêt de Brotonne."

" Ces sifflets dont il est facile de tirer un son aigu, en bouchant les extré-
mités de la fosse médullaire avec le pouce et l'index, étaient vraisemblable-
ment à l'usage des chasseurs ; cela paraît d'autant plus incontestable qu'ils
ont été trouvés avec des débris de cornes de cerf et de dents de sangliers."—
Catalogue du Musée de la Société des Antiquaires de Normandie, rédigé par M.
Gervais, p. 66.   Caen, 1864, F. Le Blanc-Hardel.

2

1

3

4

6

5

7

E. N.

B, PLATE XI.

B, PLATE XII.

these measures 8 inches in length by 6 inches in breadth, and weighs 20 lbs. (B, pl. XII. fig. 1.)

Several discs rudely formed from brick, 3 to 5 inches in diameter. These, and the two preceding ovoid-shaped stones may have probably been used by fishermen as sinkers for their nets ; or they may have been loom weights.[*]

A flat-shaped mortar in granite, measuring 10 inches in length by 8 inches in breadth, the face polished by use ; had probably been used for bruising grain or preparing food. (B, pl. XII. fig. 2.) Similar stones are to this day used by the natives of Bengal and other parts of India for preparing their food.

Another stone, in every respect similar to the former, except that on the face the mark IXII was engraved. (B, pl. XII. fig. 3.) Near this stone was found the fragment of a small bowl, having the same mark engraved on its rim after firing. (B, pl. XII. fig. 4.) It looked as if the two latter objects had been marked for some special service.

Three cylindrical stones, in granite, with the ends rounded

---

[*] " Rien de moins démontré que la véritable destination de ces objets, ordinairement en brique, quelquefois en pierre, de forme conique souvent tronquée et percés dans la partie supérieure pour donner passage à un anneau ou à une corde.

" L'opinion la plus répandue leur attribue la destination de poids à peser. Ils ont pu, tout aussi bien, servir de contre-poids ; ceux en pierre que possède le musée, et qui ont été trouvés à Vieux, n'étaient certainement que des poids d'immersion pour les grands filets de pêche connus sous le nom de seines (*sagena*)."

" La pesanteur inégale de ces cônes, rend fort problématique leur emploi usuel comme poids à peser. Il est rare, en effet, d'en rencontrer qui correspondent au poids de la livre romaine, de 6,144 grains, et à ses multiples ou divisions décimales."—*Catalogue du musée de la Société des Antiquaires de Normandie*, p. 43, rédigé par M. Gervais, conservateur. Caen, F. Le Blanc-Hardel.

off, measuring from 3 to 5 inches in length, were probably rollers or pestles which had been used with the mortars described.

Several fragments of cups in fine white glass, with striæ in relief.

A vase in black earth (reconstructed), having the form of a water goblet, the mouth widened out from the neck, in which the handle is inserted. At the base of the neck a cord in relief, and on the shoulder at the junction of the handle a frieze of enrolled ornamentation engraved hollow, between two circular lines; height 10¾ inches, breadth, 8¾ inches. (B, pl. XIII. fig. 1.)

Another vase (reconstruction) of the same form and description save that the ornament on the shoulder is formed by undulating lines, with points between the undulations. (B, pl. XIII. fig. 2.)

A deep plate or vase (reconstruction) with a hollow base, in the red lustrous ware called Samian; diameter 10¾ inches. (B, pl. XIII. fig. 3.)

Fragment of the same sort ornamented with small diamond shaped markings, obtained by moulding. (B, pl. XIII. fig. 5, natural size.)

Fragment of a bowl in the same ware, having palm leaves finely engraved. (B, pl. XIII. fig. 4.)

Fragment of the rim of a vase in the same ware, orna- mented with undulating lines; engraved free hand. This fragment is pierced by a circular hole, which appears to have been drilled after the firing. (B, pl. XIV. fig. 1.)

Vases pierced in this way with holes have been frequently found in diggings on Gallo-Roman sites. Different uses have been assigned to these vases, viz. for making cheese, for

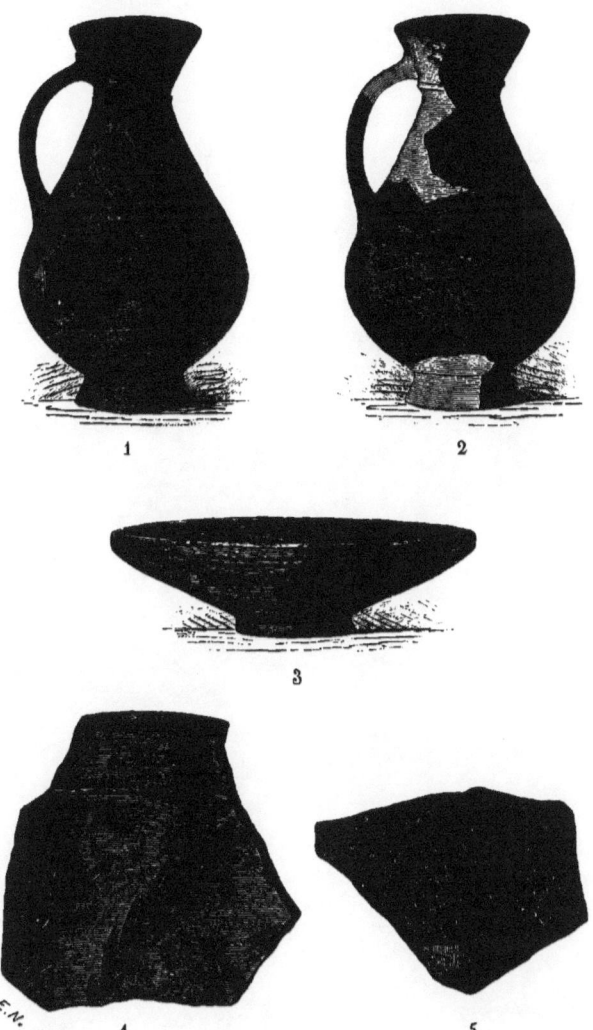

1   2

3

4   5

E. N.

To face page 48.   B, PLATE XIII.

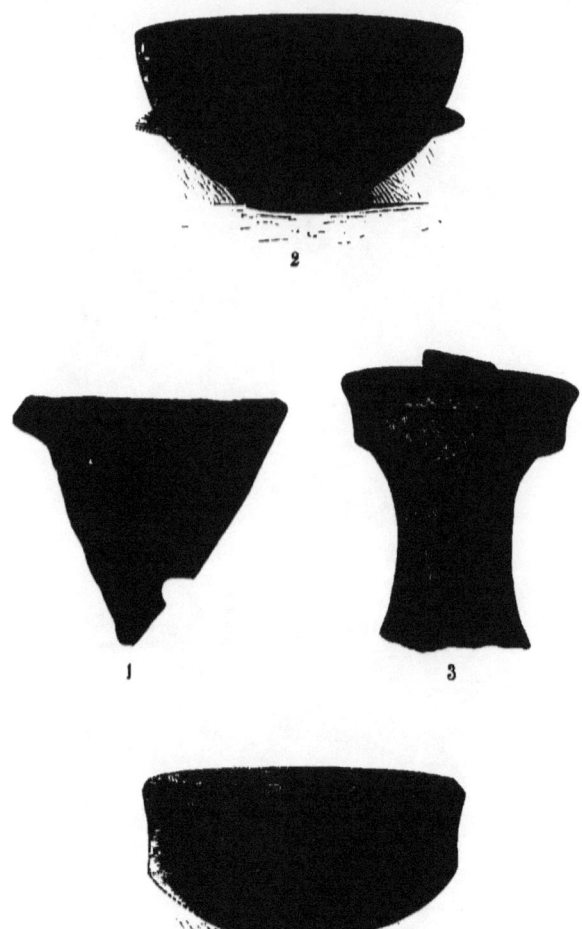

2

1   3

4

brewing beer, and for cooking purposes.   I limit myself merely to the mention of these conjectures.

A bowl (reconstructed), in brown earth, of hemispherical form, having a circular projection lapping over from the middle ; diameter 7 inches.   (B, pl. XIV. fig. 2.)

Fragment of a lamp for burning tallow or fat, in yellow earth, having an exterior rim which forms a socket.[*]   (B, pl. XIV. fig. 3.)

No traces of lamps for burning oil were found.   This at first surprised me, but I afterwards learned that they have been rarely found in this district of the Morbihan.

In the room No. 11, the only object of interest that was gathered from amidst a large quantity of tiles and pottery, was a bowl (reconstructed), in gray earth, 7 inches diameter, having vertical sides and a conical base.   (B, pl. XIV. fig. 4.)

After the digging of the Mound B had been completed, and when the different objects found in it had been classed and arranged, the curious mixture of Celtic and Roman

---

[*] " Mon lampion gaulois a été trouvé dans un antique champ de sépultures où on a enterré depuis l'époque gauloise (incinération, fosses ovoïdes), pendant tout le moyen âge et jusqu'à la Révolution ; il est, comme son confrère, en argile bien cuite, jaune-rose, modelé au tour ; le godet porte des traces de carbonisation, et en dessous une vasque formant bobèche et portant ces larges poussées qui caractérisent les poteries gauloises dans nos contrées, et qui se sont conservées sur les charniers et pones à lessive, jusqu'à nos jours.

" J'ai pu constater que toutes les sépultures gauloises par incinération, du Poitou, renfermaient un lampion à suif. Ces lampions se distinguent des lampes à huile en ce qu'ils ne portent pas de becs pour recevoir la mèche : cette distinction a été adoptée par l'habile et savant directeur du Musée de Sèvres, M. Riocreux."—*Essai sur des Poteries antiques de l'ouest de la France*, par F. Parenteau. Nantes, Henri Charpentier, 1865, p. 7.

E

pottery presented a striking appearance, and represented a remarkable variety of forms, especially in the shapes of the rims.

Seven baskets full of fragments of pottery had been collected in this mound which weighed 159 lbs. net.

DOOR AT BOURGEREL.
(From a drawing by M. Huray.)

IV.

EXCAVATIONS IN THE MOUND C.

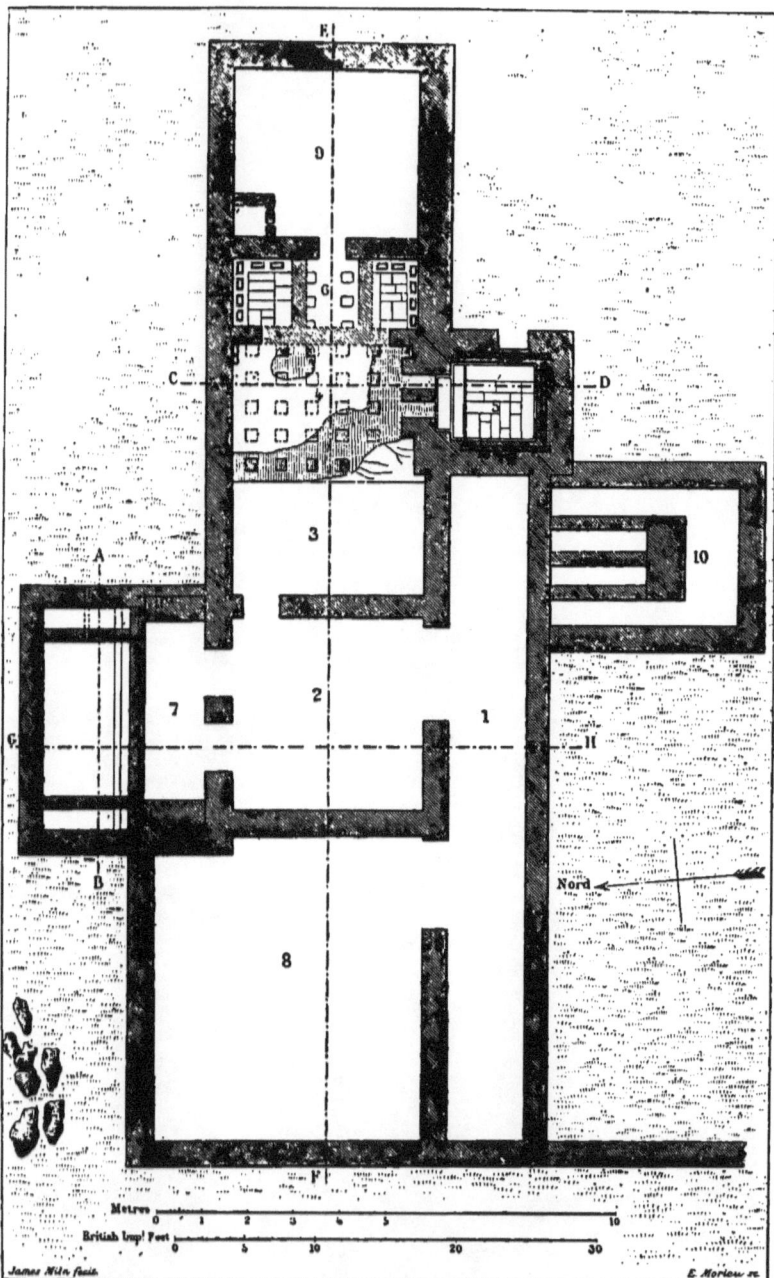

To face page 53.　　　C, PLATE I.—PLAN OF THE BATHS, MOUND C.

THE MOUND C.

As has been already mentioned in the preceding chapter, the west wall of the habitation discovered under the Mound B was found to be prolonged northwards until it joined on to another mound designated in the plan of the Bossenno by the letter C.

The Mound C was of an oval form, and had a medium height of 5 feet. Its greater axis, from east to west, measured 82 feet, and its lesser axis, from north to south, 46 feet. The exterior coating of this mound consisted of stones, earth, fragments of pottery, bricks, and tiles. We commenced work on the north side.

The result of almost the first few blows of the pick was to bring to light a quantity of the shells of edible molluscs, viz. oysters, whelks, and mussels. Shortly afterwards a hollow tile or conduit brick, 18 inches long, ornamented with five grooves* in the form of a St. Andrew's cross, was turned up.

The discovery of this conduit brick was very pleasing, for

* It was afterwards seen that these grooves served a double purpose—sometimes as ornaments, at others for the adhesion of the plaster or mortar.

E 2

it at once gave rise to the hope that we were about to find a
Gallo-Roman bathing establishment under the Mound C.
These expectations were fully justified by the result of the
diggings.   This may be seen on referring to the adjoining
ground-plan of the ruins discovered under the Mound C.

On making a careful examination of this building it becomes evident that it contains, and in their proper order, all
the rooms which, according to Messrs. de Caumont and Rich,
were required for a *Balneum*, viz., 1st, the *Apodyterium ;* 2d,
the *Tepidarium ;* 3d, the *Sudatorium ;* 4th, the *Caldarium ;* 5th,
the *Frigidarium* containing its *Baptisterium*.

The small size of the different rooms of this establishment,
the impossibility of giving separate baths for males and females,
as was always found in the public baths, makes me suppose
that here we have discovered a *Balneum* or private bath
forming a dependence of the villa found under the Mound B,
which has just been described in the preceding chapter.

What leads me to believe that any other conclusion is
untenable is that the west wall of the villa and the west wall of
the baths form one and the same wall, and are of identical construction.   (See the general plan of the Bossenno.)

Of the south wall, near the letter H of the ground-plan,
there remained little more than the foundations.   What seemed
to have been a wide entrance could here be made out, not
sufficiently distinct to admit of its being laid down on the
ground-plan, but still leaving the impression that it was the
place by which access was had from the court into the
passage No. 1.

As in the constructions found under the Mounds A and B,
so in all the parts of this building, the proofs of the fire which
had destroyed all these edifices were everywhere abundant.

In order to avoid repetition, I will henceforth give to each

room the number which it bears on the plan, also the name
by which, according to its destination, it was designated by
the Romans.

The passage No. 1 measured 47 feet in length by 5 feet
6 inches in breadth, and gave access by two doorways to the
rooms Nos. 2 and 8. The floor was formed of cement, as
were all the floors of the different parts of this building
excepting the room No. 9. As has been already mentioned,
the traces of a large doorway, which had been the principal
entrance to the baths, were visible in the south wall near
the letter H, but were not sufficiently distinct to admit of
their being laid down on the plan.

The room No. 2 appears to me to have been the *Apodyterium** where the bathers undressed and deposited their
clothes. It forms a square measuring 13 feet 6 inches of a
side. The remains of the four walls had an average height of
3 feet 4 inches. On the north side are two doorways communicating with the *Frigidarium*, No. 7, and on the east side
a doorway giving access to the room No. 3. The regularity
of the courses and excellence of construction of these walls
excited the attention and admiration not only of my workmen
but also of the numerous visitors who came to see the
diggings.

Some portions of the walls had a coating of plaster, decorated, at three feet from the floor, with a red band two inches
in breadth.

Underneath the cement which formed the floor was a

---

* *Apodyterium* An undressing-room ; especially a chamber in the baths,
where the visitors undressed and left their clothes whilst bathing.—*Dictionary
of Roman and Greek Antiquities*, by Anthony Rich. London, 1860. Longman.

deep bed of small round stones, having a few pieces of charcoal and pottery interspersed. This bed appeared to have
been prepared so as to form a medium of drainage for the
apartment. On digging down to a depth of six feet the
natural soil was not reached.

The room No. 3 measured 13 feet 6 inches in length by
8 feet 3 inches in breadth.

In the middle of this room we came upon a long bench
formed of cement, but in a very soft and dilapidated condition:
notwithstanding all the care that was taken for its preservation,
it fell to pieces on being exposed to the air. Several polished
slabs in a fine white calcareous stone were embedded on the
upper face, and five pieces of marble slabs, white veined with
red, scattered on the floor, were probably the remnants of
what had once been the covering of this bench. This room
appeared to me to have been the *Elæothesium*,* and that it was
on the bench above described that the bather placed himself
in order to be rubbed, manipulated with strigils, and anointed.
This supposition was so far strengthened by our having afterwards discovered, when clearing the south wall, numerous
fragments of vases, in a recess there, which may have been
the place for keeping the oils and ointments with which the
bather was anointed after he had been rubbed and manipulated.

On the floor a few feeble traces remained of a thin partition, separating this room from the *Tepidarium*,† No. 4. It is

---

* *Elæothesium.* The oiling-room in a set of baths, where the oils and
unguents were kept, and to which the bather retired to be rubbed and
anointed.—*Dictionary.* A. Rich.

† *Tepidarium.* A chamber in a set of baths kept at a moderate degree
of temperature, in order to prepare the body for the great heat of the *Suda-*

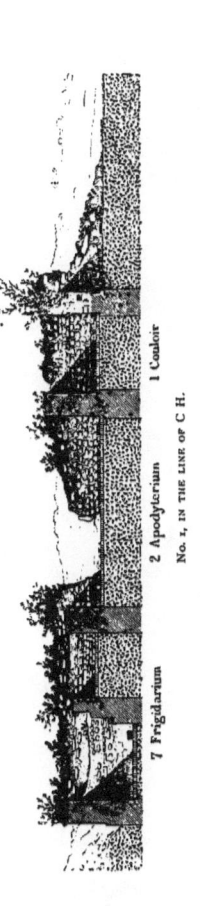

7 Frigidarium   2 Apodyterium   1 Couloir

No. 1, IN THE LINE OF C H.

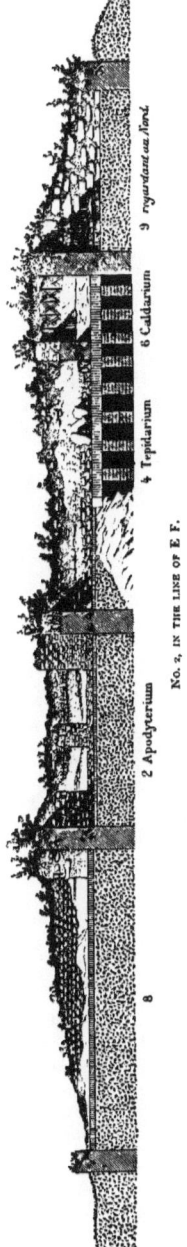

2 Apodyterium   4 Tepidarium   6 Caldarium   9 *regardant au Nord*

No. 2, IN THE LINE OF E F.

8

Sudatorium   Tepidarium *regardant à l'Ouest*

No. 3, IN THE LINE OF C D.

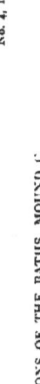

Baptisterium *dans le Frigidarium regardant au Nord*

No. 4, IN THE LINE OF A B.

C, PLATE III.—SECTIONS OF THE BATHS, MOUND C.

To face page 56.

quite possible that the rooms No. 3 and 4 may have had large openings in the partition between them, so as to be considered as forming only one apartment. This was, besides, the most usual arrangement in the private baths; according to Rich, the *Elæothesium* and the *Tepidarium* often formed one and the same room.

The room No. 4 measured 13 feet in length, by 9 feet 6 inches in breadth. The floor, formed of a bed of a red-coloured cement 9 inches in thickness, had been covered with large polished slabs of bluish-gray schist. Several of these remained imbedded in the cement, which also bore the impress of those that were wanting.

Under this bed of cement a hypocaust was discovered, having square pillars 2 feet 2 inches in height, placed at a distance of 16 inches from each other. These pillars were formed of bricks, measuring 8 and 9 inches square, set in a thick bed of mortar.

The hypocaust was choked up with soot, charcoal, cinders, and earth, mingled with a few fragments of pottery.

Two steps, rudely cut in the rock, were discovered in the south-west corner, near the *Sudatorium;* the use of these is not quite apparent.

In the north-west corner two vertical flues formed of hollow bricks, similar to the one found at the commencement of the diggings, and figured at page 53, served to convey the heated air from the hypocaust.

There can be little doubt as to the destination of the room No. 4; it was the *Tepidarium*, a room kept at a moderate temperature. The communication from this room to No.

torium or vapour bath, and to break the sudden transition after it, before returning into the open air.—*Dictionary.*   A. Rich.

5 was by a small stair, of which a few steps remained when the diggings were executed.

The room No. 5, nearly square in form, measured 5 feet in length by 4 feet 8 inches in breadth. Its destination was not evident until it had been completely cleared out, when it became apparent that it was the *Sudatorium* [*] or *Sudatio con-camerata*. The height of the walls on the north, south, and east side was 6 feet 8 inches, on the west side 7 feet 6 inches. It was constructed over a hypocaust, and was supported by five square pillars. The floor and the walls were faced with polished slabs of blue slate. Two steps, superposed, had been worked into the north wall; these also were faced with polished slate.

Double rows of flues, formed of hollow bricks, ascending through the walls from the hypocaust below, served to circulate the heated air. These hollow bricks, as may be seen on referring to the section C D, were supported by crotchet tiles, *tegulæ*, fastened by iron double-headed nails driven into the mortar, and covered over all by a layer of cement and by the facing of polished slate already mentioned. This arrangement of flues was not broken into on the south wall, as I always endeavoured, whilst disengaging these ruins, to preserve them as much as possible intact. The system for circulating the heated air was besides perfectly shown in the east and west walls.

In the bottom of this small room, a lead pipe, passing through the south wall at the level of the floor, had served to run off the condensed water.

[*] *Sudatorium.* The sudatory or sweating-room in a set of baths, which was heated by flues arranged under the flooring (*suspensura*), and sometimes also constructed in the walls of the chamber, when it was specially termed *Sudatio concamerata.—Dictionary.* A. Rich.

G. PLATE IV. INTERIOR OF THE BATHS, SHOWING THE HYPOCAUST.

A granite stone pillar was let into slabs of slate forming the floor, so as to make a pedestal or seat. Facing this pillar, in the east wall, was a recess, having an opening 8 inches wide, which may have served to regulate the temperature, or to admit fresh air from the exterior at the will of the bather.

The room No. 6 measured 13 feet in length by 5 feet in breadth, and, like the rooms Nos. 4 and 5, was also constructed over a hypocaust.

A small bath or reservoir for holding warm water, measuring 3 feet 6 inches in length by 2 feet 9 inches in breadth, was discovered on clearing out the north side of this room. Another bath of the same kind, measuring 3 feet 10 inches by 2 feet 6 inches, was found on the south side.

The bottoms of these baths were laid with polished slabs of a fine white calcareous stone, which is not found in the environs of Carnac. The sides were faced with polished slabs of blue slate.

Round the sides of each bath six vertical flues, formed of hollow bricks, served to convey the heated air from the hypocaust below, and to warm the water.

The situation and arrangement of this chamber indicate its having been the *Caldarium*,* or room into which the bather passed from the *Sudatorium* to be washed with hot water after the action of the hot-air bath had induced a sufficient perspiration.

A reference to the ground-plan of the Mound C will show that the flooring between the baths just described had fallen in ruins, and thereby exposed the pillars of the hypocaust below. According to Rich, the *Labrum* would have been situated between these baths, but nothing was found there save some

* *Caldarium.* The thermal chamber in a set of baths.—*Dictionary.* A. Rich.

fragments of a large vase and a few curious pieces of frescoes decorated with shells, one of which is figured in the chromo-lithograph C, pl. VI.

The general aspect and character of this room denoted that great care had been bestowed on its construction, and it was still in a good state of preservation when first cleared out. Unfortunately, numbers of tourists and country people came to see the ruins. They soon carried off the fine white stones of the baths, stripped and overset the walls, and demolished the pillars of the hypocaust.

The room No. 7 measured 15 feet in length by 11 feet 6 inches in breadth. It contained on the north side a cold bath or *Baptisterium*,* having reservoirs for cold water at each end.

The cold bath measured 10 feet 6 inches in length by 5 feet in breadth. Its depth below the level of the floor of the room was 4 feet. A conduit passing through the east wall, at the bottom of the bath, had served to run off the waste water. Two steps, superposed, were worked into the south side; the first at 1 foot 8 inches, the second at 3 feet 11 inches from the bottom, destined, probably, to assist the bather in ascending and descending. The sides and bottom were formed of a thick coat of cement. See the section No. 1, G H, C pl. III.

The reservoirs or cisterns measured each 5 feet in length by 1 foot 6 inches in breadth. The depth of the reservoir situated at the west end of the bath was 4 feet 10 inches, whilst that at the east end was only 3 feet 4 inches. This difference is caused by the conduit or discharge pipe from the bottom of the bath passing below the latter reservoir. See the section No. 4, A B, C pl. III.

* *Baptisterium.* A cold plunging bath constructed in the *cella frigidaria.* —*Dictionary.* A. Rich.

The sides of the two reservoirs were faced with cement only, whilst the bottoms were carefully laid with slate embedded in cement.

On ascending from the bath to the room above, another conduit is to be seen in the section No. 1, G H, passing through the east wall at the level of the floor, and serving to run off the water used by the bather : two seats or benches were worked into the walls—one on the east, the other on the west side.

The construction here leaves but little doubt that it was the room called by the Romans the *Frigidarium.*[*]

Two doorways on the south side, separated by a square pillar, gave access to it from the *Apodyterium.*

When the clearing out of this room was completed, the pillar was in a good state of preservation, faced with plaster, on which a red band, $1\frac{1}{4}$ inch in breadth, was painted 16 inches from the floor.

In clearing out the debris which choked up this room, numerous fragments of curious frescoes were discovered. These appeared to me to have been the remains of what had once formed the ceiling of the *Frigidarium,* and which had fallen down at the time of its destruction.

The greater portion of these fragments were quite soft and friable, so much so that many had to be sacrificed in order to extricate a single specimen.

These fragments, as may be seen on referring to the accompanying chromo-lithographs, were painted in geometric designs red, blue, green, yellow, and white ; decorated with shells embedded in the plaster. Many of these shells were

* *Frigidarium.* It was certainly distinct from the cold-water bath (*frigido lavatio*), with which it was enumerated, but situated in an opposite angle of the edifice and adjoining the oiling-room (*Elæothesium*).

broken, and had fallen off the plaster.   In some instances the
place which they had occupied on the plaster bore no trace of
colour, which shows that they had been placed on the plaster
before it was painted.

The marks of the compasses used by the painter in working
out his design were still visible on some of the fragments.   I
mention this on account of a remark made by many of the
numerous visitors who came to see the collection of objects
discovered in the course of the diggings.   A pair of iron
compasses was found in the Mound D, which they declared
to be an instrument of comparatively modern date, and they
also stated that it was doubtful if compasses were known
in Brittany during the Roman occupation.   On seeing
the marks on the fragments above alluded to they at once
acknowledged their error.*

The colours of these fragments were bright and clear when
found, but after a few days' exposure they became dull and
faint.

With the view of simplifying the description of these
frescoes and of the reconstruction of the design of the ceiling,
I shall first direct the attention of the reader to some of the
more important specimens, as shown in the three chromo-
lithographs which follow.

1. Fragment of plaster, the decoration formed of parallel
bands, containing geometric figures in polychrome, with shells
of different species inserted.   (Chromo-lithograph C, pl. V.,
natural size.)

2. Fragment of plaster, the decoration formed of undulating bands in polychrome, having shells embedded.
(Chromo-lithograph C, pl. VI., natural size.)

---

* *Circinus.*   A pair of compasses employed by carpenters, architects,
masons, and sculptors, for describing circles, etc. etc., similar to those still in
use.—*Dictionary.* A. Rich.

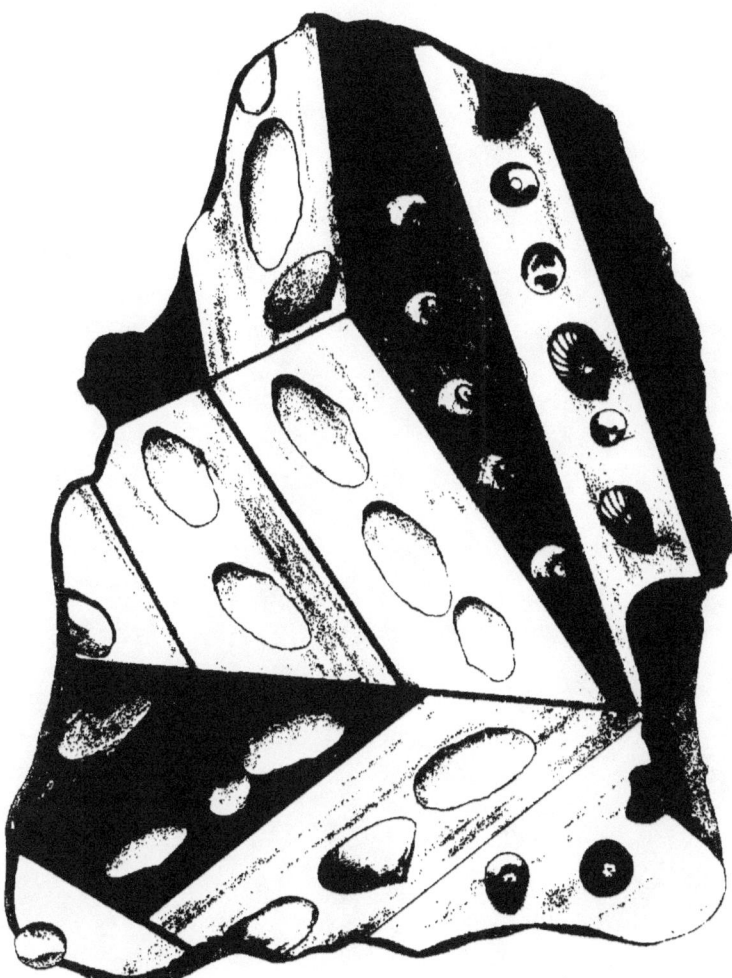

Imp. Leroy & Richon, Paris.

L. Cappe. Del.

.C. PLATE V.—FRAGMENT OF CEILING IN FRESCO (ACTUAL SIZE).

To face page 60.

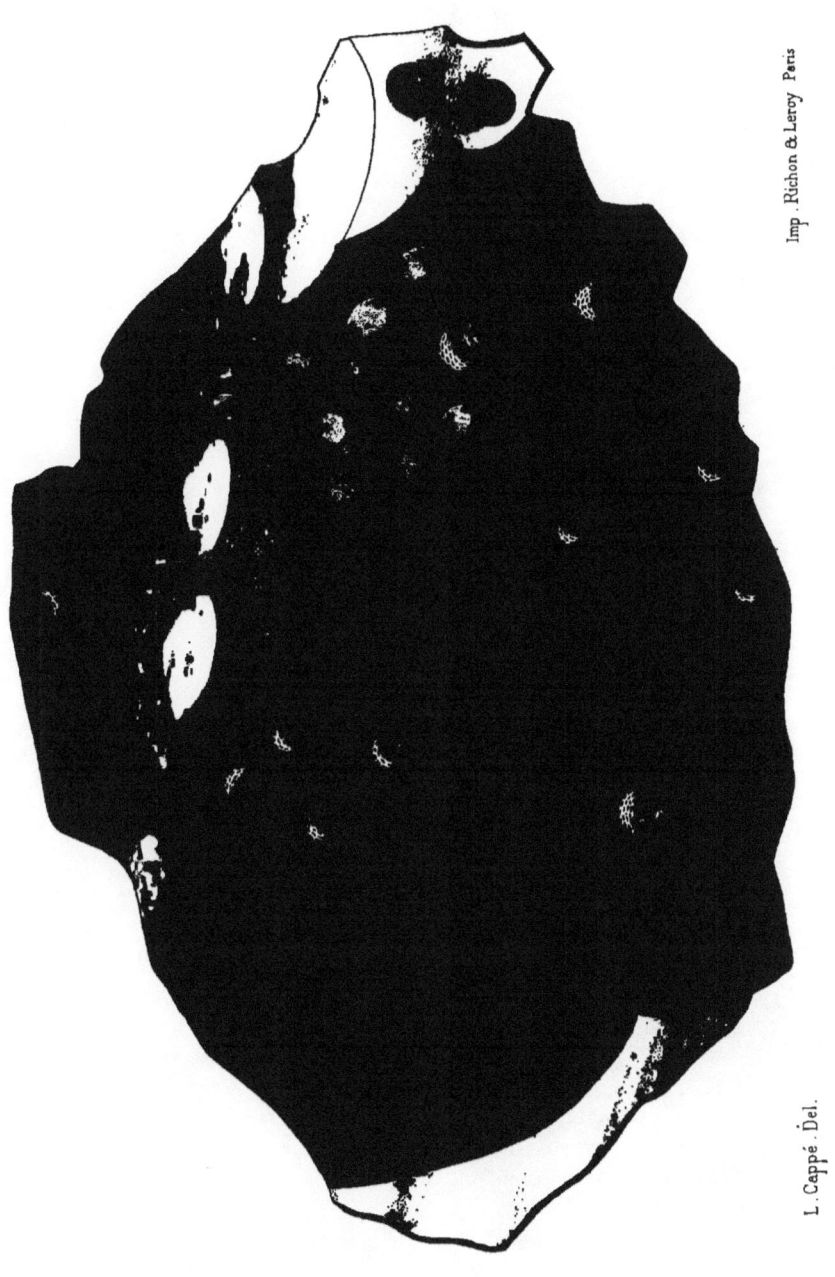

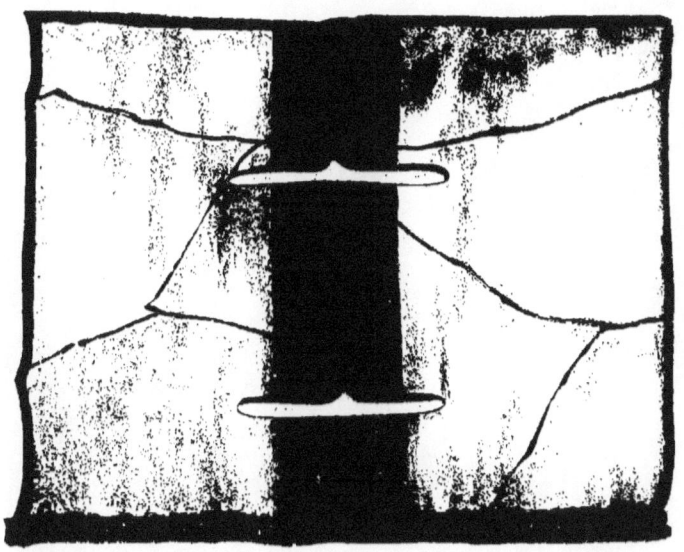

PL . 4

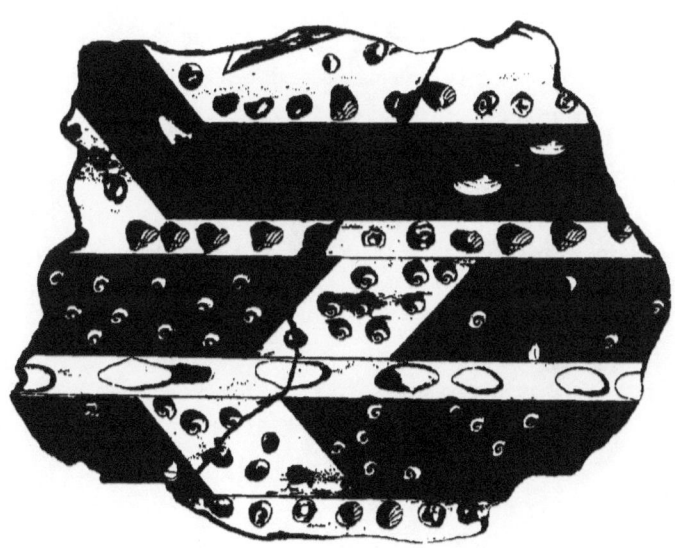

Cappé . Del.

Imp . Leroy & Richon . Paris

To face page 62, 3d.   C, PLATE VII.
PART OF WINDOW AND OF CEILING (Reduced).

3. Fragment of plaster, the decoration in polychrome, forming part of a border surrounding an octagonal design, having shells embedded. (Chromo-lithograph C, pl. VII. fig. 4, half size.)

The different fragments discovered, of which these three chromos afford fair specimens, enabled me, with the aid of M. Henry du Cleuziou and M. Louis Cappé, to reproduce the decoration of certain portions of the ceiling, which are represented in the following chromos.

1. Part of the ceiling reconstructed, the decoration in polychrome, composed of a rosace surrounded by an octagon. The central part of the rosace is divided into eight compartments of varied colours ; over the whole shells of the genus *turbo* and *tellina* are embedded. (Chromo C, pl. VIII. fig. 9.)

2. One of the original fragments made use of for the preceding reconstruction. (Chromo C, pl. VIII. fig. 10, reduced one half.)

3. Part of the border of the ceiling reconstructed, the decoration in polychrome, composed of a large yellow band, having shells of the *Cardium echinatum* embedded, and of other smaller bands in various colours divided into compartments, with shells of the *turbo* and *tellina* embedded. (Chromo C, pl. IX., reduced one fourth.)

4. Part of the ceiling restored, the decoration in polychrome, containing a diamond-shaped figure divided into compartments, in which are embedded shells of the *Cardium echinatum*, *turbo*, and *tellina*. (Chromo C, pl. X.)

M. H. du Cleuziou, after studying the combinations that could be obtained with these fragments, succeeded in making a design of the entire ceiling.

M. L. Cappé, in following the same method but making use

of other fragments subsequently found, made the reconstruction represented in C, pl. XI., which I believe to be more exact.

I regret that the size of this volume does not admit of his design being given on a large scale in chromo.

Several fragments of frescoes similar to those just described were discovered a few years ago by M. R. F. le Men, when excavating the Gallo-Roman baths at Poul-Ker, near Ben-Odet, below the town of Quimper. Specimens of these are exhibited in the museum at Quimper.

The apartment No. 8 probably served as a waiting-room for the bather until the bath was ready, or for repose after taking it. The entrance was by the doorway in the south wall.

The average height of the walls was on the north side 2 feet 6 inches, on the south 4 feet, on the west 3 feet. On the east side the foundation alone remained.

These remains of walls were in good preservation and had a coating of plaster still preserving some traces of painting. On the north wall, at the height of 10 inches from the floor, and on the right hand, was a horizontal red band 6 inches in breadth. In the middle of the wall this was replaced by a yellow band 6 inches in breadth; 8 inches higher there was another red band of the same breadth.

On the east wall traces were found of green leaves painted on a white ground, and of a red sort of fruit on a black ground. (Chromo B, pl. V.)

Specimens of plaster similar to those here described, and found in different Roman and Gallo-Roman establishments, are exhibited in the museums at London, Paris, etc. etc. It would seem that the most common style of mural decoration in the Gallo-Roman epoch consisted of bands in primitive colours painted on a white ground.

L. Cappé. Del.

To face page 64.

C. PLATE VIII.—FRAGMENT IN FRESCO AND RECONSTRUCTION.

Imp. Leroy & Richon. Paris.

C, PLATE IX.

RECONSTRUCTION, BORDER OF CEILING IN FRESCO.

Pl. 6.

To face page 14, 3d. C, PLATE X.

RECONSTRUCTION, PART OF CEILING IN FRESCO.

C, PLATE XI.

RECONSTRUCTION, DESIGN OF CEILING.

E. Morieu sc.

The floor of this apartment was formed of a bed of fine smooth cement, which gave a hollow sound on walking over it. On digging down below it for some distance, nothing was found but small stones laid for drainage in the same way as below the *Apodyterium*.

The room No. 9 measured 13 feet in length by 12 feet in breadth. The walls were constructed with irregularly-shaped stones of different sizes, in inferior workmanship, and had no coating of plaster. The floor was without cement. It seems to me that this room had been intended for the use of the slaves who attended on the baths, more especially for those who attended to the heating. The furnace whence the heat was distributed through the baths was placed in the middle of the west wall. In the north-west corner there was a square construction, which appeared to have been the chimney. Several visitors suggested that the room No. 9 had been an open court, but the quantity of roofing tiles found on clearing out the floor showed that it had been roofed in part, if not entirely.

The construction No. 10 was an enigma to all who saw it. It had no connection with the baths, although it was joined on to them. It was situated at a depth of 2 feet 8 inches under the pasture which exists between the Mounds B and C, already alluded to as a court. Three or four courses of rude masonry in irregularly shaped stones were all that remained of its surrounding walls. In the middle were two vaulted constructions which appeared to have been furnaces, measuring 3 feet in length by 1 foot 8 inches in width. One of these was filled with charcoal, ashes, and earth, the other with lime and pounded brick dust.

F

Various ideas as to the use of this construction suggested themselves.

Seeing that it was below the level of the floors of either the villa or the baths, might it not have been the place where the cement, which would be required in large quantities, had been prepared anterior to the building of these edifices, and which had been covered over after their completion? Or might it have been used for firing the tiles or coarse pottery required for the use of the establishment? This, however, could hardly have been agreeable to the inhabitants of such a luxurious dwelling. Seeing that none of its masonry bears any trace of Roman workmanship, it may have been constructed after the destruction of the Bossenno, for some purpose now unknown; but whatever its destination may have been, the workmen gave it the name of the Furnaces, which it retained. (C, pl. XII.)

Having now finished the description of the various parts of the building discovered under the Mound C, I shall proceed with the enumeration of the different objects found in it, commencing with those found on the outside of the walls.

On the north-east face of the mound, near the place where the conduit tile mentioned at the commencement of this chapter was found, a number of square tiles were collected, ornamented with hollow lines, forming concentric circular figures, ovals, and diamond-shaped patterns. Similar tiles found in the Roman ruins at Carhaix and Benodet are exhibited in the museum of Quimper, one of which is represented in the engraving at the end of this chapter (page 73).

At the foot of the north wall of the room No. 4, on the outside of the building, was a large quantity of broken window-

To face page 160.

G. PLATE XII   FURNACES BESIDE THE BATHS

glass of a green colour, having one face polished, and the other rough as if it had been cast on sand. On the border of some of the fragments a line of red cement still remained. Alongside of these was an iron bar furnished with cross pieces in lead. (C, pl. XIII. fig. 1.) These were the remains of a window which had been broken at the time of the destruction of the building. The chromo-lithograph C, pl. VII. No. 2, represents the reconstruction of a portion of this window.

At a distance of about five feet from the wall of the room No. 4 there was found a small bronze coin of Constantine the Great, in a good state of preservation :—

CONSTANTINVS. AVG. Bust turned to the left, crowned with laurel, having the imperial mantle, and holding a sceptre surmounted by an eagle.

Reverse: BEATA. TRANQVILLITAS. An altar surmounted by a globe, above which are three stars : on the altar VOTIS XX. (Cohen, 193.)

Several fragments of red lustrous ware, and of an amphora in yellow earth, were found at a short distance from the north side of the wall of the room No. 9. All the earth turned up here was passed through sieves, with the view of collecting all the fragments of a vase similar to those already mentioned as having been found in London. It required a good deal of perseverance to select, adapt, and cement these different fragments, so as to complete the reconstruction of this vase, which is represented in the chromo-lithograph A, pl. IV.

There were also found here a small bronze ring like a marriage-ring, the head of a bronze button or ornament of hemispherical form similar to the one found in the Mound A, several iron nails of different sizes, and a few fragments of wall plaster painted red.

In digging round the exterior of the *Sudatorium*, a large bronze coin of Lucilla Augusta was found on the east side, near to the foot of the walls of No. 9 :—

LVCILLÆ. AVG. ANTONINI. AVG. F. (Lucillæ Augustæ Antonini Augusti filiæ). Bust turned to the right.

Reverse : VENVS. S. C. (Venus senatus consulto.) Venus erect, turned to the left, holding an apple and a sceptre. (Cohen, 79.)

Near the south-east corner of the *Sudatorium* we came upon an antler of the common red deer (*Cervus elaphus*), and several fragments of deers' horns broken and cut.

The teeth, ribs, and other bones of oxen, which had been of a small race.

Bones and teeth of the sheep.

Jaw-bones complete with teeth, and tibia of the red deer (*Cervus elaphus*).

Boars' tusks ; teeth and bones of the pig.

Bones of hares and rabbits.

Mingled with these bones were the débris of edible shell-fish, viz.—

The whelk	(*Buccinum undatum*).
Oyster	(*Ostrea edulis*).
Limpet .	(*Patella vulgata*).
Scallop or palmer shell	(*Pecten Jacobeus*).
Ormer	(*Haliotis tubercularis*).
Mussel	(*Mytilus edulis*).
Snail	(*Helix pomatica.*)

Mr. Wright, in his work *The Celt, Roman, and Saxon*, refers to the fact that the proximity of Roman sites in England is almost always shown by the presence of immense quantities of the shells of the oyster, cockle, and mussel. He also mentions the curious circumstance that a large species of snail is often found still existing about Roman stations.

The manufactured articles found here were—

Part of a tool in tempered steel.

Numerous fragments of Gallo-Roman pottery, consisting of pieces of handles, bottoms, and rims of vases in red, gray, and black earth.

In the interior of the building there were found in the passage No. 1 several fragments of common gray pottery, and also of a plate in red ware.

In the *Apodyterium*, No. 2, only a few fragments of very coarse pottery.

In the *Elæothesium* and *Tepidarium*, Nos. 3 and 4, several flakes of black flint, a flat hone or sharpening-stone, and numerous fragments of pottery of different kinds. Amongst these were the bottom of a tripod bowl in the red ware, called false Samian. In the whole course of the diggings only one other tripod bowl was found, viz. in the Mound A. Some of the fragments were in common gray earth, ornamented with a series of circular horizontal bands painted black.

In the *Sudatorium*, No. 5, nothing was found save a quantity of bricks, tiles, and earth.

In the *Caldarium*, No. 6, there were two bodkins formed of deer's horn, each two inches in length.

Two fragments of a marble slab, blue with white veins.

Fragments of a large vase in gray earth, which enabled me to reconstruct the upper half of a vase similar to that figured B, pl. VII. fig. 2.

In the *Frigidarium*, No. 7, several burnt bones were found in the cold bath, also a tool formed from a deer's horn, having the point bevelled off, and several fragments of small vases in fine black lustrous ware.

In the room No. 8, near the centre, a penannular brooch of Celtic type in bronze, formed from a flat ring, having a simple but not ungraceful ornament engraved on the upper flat of the ring, and having a short pin.   (C, pl. XIII. fig. 3, natural size.)

A small armlet in plain thin bronze wire.

In the north-east corner, the neck of a small bottle in clear glass.

A small opaque bead of a turquoise blue colour, half an inch in diameter, probably part of a necklace.

Several iron nails and pieces of iron of different forms—use unknown.

Piece of a steel drill, similar to the drills used by carpenters at the present time.   (C, pl. XIII. fig. 4, natural size.)

Fragment of a marble slab, white with red veins.

The different marbles found at the Bossenno were submitted to the inspection of experts in London and Paris, with the view of ascertaining the locality from which they had been brought.   They declined to give a decided opinion, seeing that they had marbles exactly similar, found both in Italy and in Africa, of which they produced specimens. This is an interesting question, for as there are no quarries of marble in the Morbihan, and as marbles have been

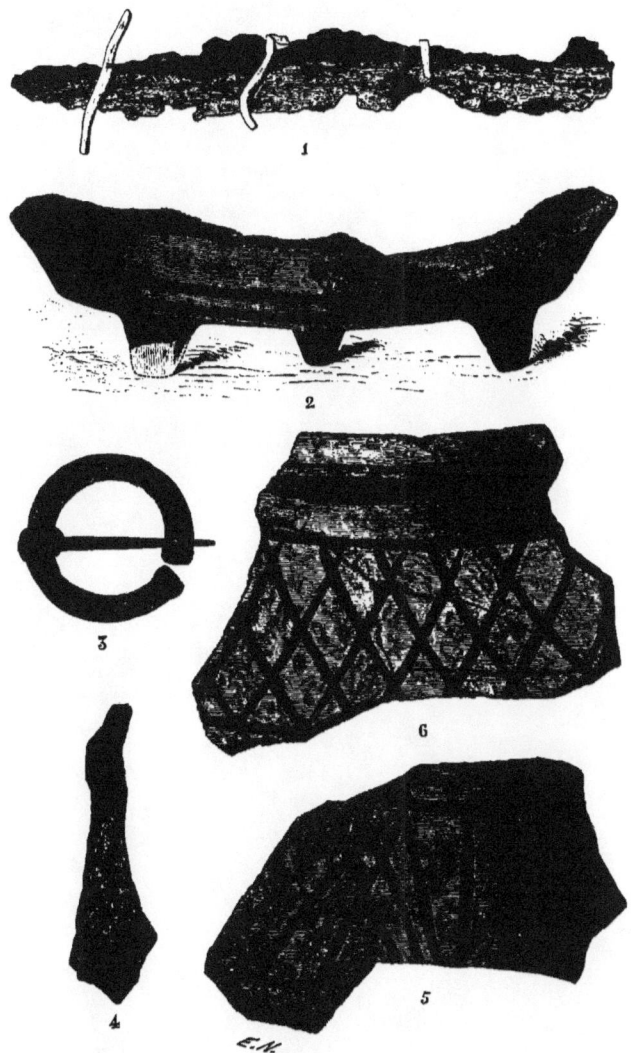

1

2

3

6

4

5

E.N.

C, PLATE XIII.

frequently found in excavating the Roman ruins of that department, it points to a foreign commerce of some extent during the Roman occupation.[*]

Several whorls in terra-cotta, and one made out of a piece of blue slate, were found scattered on the floor. These had been placed on a wooden spindle and used for spinning thread. To this day in Brittany, the women watching their flocks on the moorlands may be seen spinning in this way. Whorls exactly similar have been used till quite recently in some parts of the Highlands of Scotland, and in Shetland.

Several of these found during the course of the diggings at the Bossenno were not pierced in the centre, but had an

oblique perforation near the edge; this precludes the idea of their having been used for spinning purposes. Perhaps they may have been used as weavers' weights, or sinkers for nets or fishing-lines. Stone sinkers similar to these, though of larger size, are still used by the Shetland fishermen.

[*] "Il n'existe donc du terrain de transition, dans le Morbihan, que deux étages, le Cambrien et le Silurien, séparés l'un de l'autre par l'éruption des granits à petits éléments. L'étage cambrien est formé de grès à grains, fins, de schiste talqueux ou chloritiques et de mica schistes staurotidifères."

"L'étage silurien comprend le gneiss, les poudingues, les quartzites, les schistes argileux, les grauwaches schisteux et les mica schistes maclifères."— *Bulletin de la Société Polymathique du Morbihan*, pour l'année 1860.

Several pieces of tiles ornamented in the same manner as those found on the north-east side of the Mound C were found in clearing out this room; also several fragments of pottery in common gray earth, in fine black earth having a lustrous glazing, in red lustrous ware, and rims, bottoms, and handles of vases of varied sorts. From all these fragments only one vase could be reconstructed, a hollow dish in common gray earth similar to that described in the Mound A. (A, pl. III. fig 5).

In the room No. 9, near the south-east corner, were a quantity of rounded pieces of tiles, from 3 to 4 inches in diameter, probably sinkers or pieces for playing at some game. To this day, in Brittany, the game of *palét* is a favourite amusement. The workmen, on finding the rounded pieces of tile, exclaimed, "They played at palét then, these ancients as we do now." The earth and stones cleared out here were, as in all the other rooms, mixed with numerous fragments of bricks and roofing tiles, *tegulæ* and *imbrices*. Near the base of the north wall were a few small fragments of wall plaster, coloured red and yellow, which had probably fallen from the adjoining room at the time of the destruction of the building.

Near the north-east corner was a small bronze coin, slightly degraded, of Constantius the Second.

D. N. CONSTANTIVS. P. F. AVG. (Dominus noster Constantius pius, felix Augustus.) Bust to the right; diadem and paludamentum.

Reverse: FEL. TEMP. REPARATIO. (Felix temporum reparatio.) Soldier in a fury, erect to the left, piercing with his spear and spurning with his foot an enemy who, holding a shield, has fallen below his horse in endeavouring to hold on to the mane. A shield on the earth. (Cohen, 223.)

Near to the east wall were several iron nails of different sizes, also three implements in steel, resembling punches and drills.

Numerous fragments of coarse pottery enabled me to reconstruct a flat deep dish, already described as *er cass*, and another, 8 inches in diameter, pear-shaped, in gray-brown earth, with black bands. Several fragments of vases, in gray earth, similar to those described in the Mound A, having a decoration resembling Moorish pottery, were also found in this room ; specimens of these are represented, C, pl. XIII. figs. 5 and 6.

The fragments of pottery collected in the Mound C filled five baskets, and weighed 143 lbs.

TILE FOUND AT CARHAIX.

V.

EXCAVATIONS IN THE MOUND D.

THE MOUND D.

BEARING in mind that the Romans generally placed a temple, dedicated to Venus or Mars, in the vicinity of their baths; so soon as the exploration of the Mound C was terminated, I sought all round for traces of a building that might have had such a destination.

There seemed to be some prospect of finding this (taking into account the persistence of names and traditions in Brittany), when I learned from the peasants that the Mounds D and E were known in the country by the name of the temple. This statement was confirmed by my workmen.

On placing poles some distance apart on the north wall of the baths, it could be seen that the southern face of the Mound D was in the prolongation of a line drawn through these poles. On digging holes in this line, in the cultivated land between the Mounds C and D, the foundations of the wall which united the baths to the building buried under the Mound D were discovered.

The excavation of the Mound D was commenced on the 14th July 1875, and abundant proofs were soon found that it covered the ruins of a small temple or *Lararium*.*

---

* *Lararium*. A sort of shrine, small chapel, or apartment, where the statues of the *Lares* or guardian spirits of a household, as well as other sanctified or deified personages, were placed and worshipped.—Lamprid, *Alex. Sev.*, 29

This little mound was of a roundish form, and almost flat:
it measured 44 feet in diameter and 2 feet in height.   In
appearance it was so insignificant as to cause it to be overlooked at first, when searching for indications of a temple, but
the results obtained from its exploration were of great interest.

Work was commenced on the south side, and in a short
space of time a wall was struck upon, right in the prolongation of the line indicated by the poles.   We continued working round the Mound, following and clearing the outside of
the wall until the ruins of a square building, measuring 32
feet 6 inches of a side, about 2 feet in height, and having an
entrance from the south, were completely exposed to view.
The clearing out of the interior was then proceeded with, and
soon disclosed the remains of another square building, measuring 14 feet of a side, about 2 feet in height, with walls 31
inches in breadth, and without any entrance.   These two
constructions represented (see the ground-plan of the Mound
D) two squares, one within the other, having a free passage
8 feet wide between their four sides.   On the floor of the
inner square, at a distance of 2 feet from the north wall a
slab of fine white calcareous stone, 2 feet 3 inches square, 3
inches in thickness, and having mouldings cut on three sides,
was found embedded in a layer of cement.   It appeared to me
that this had served as the base of a pedestal on which had
been placed the statue of the divinity to whom this little
temple had been dedicated.

As the walls surrounding the inner square showed no
indication of an entrance, it may be supposed that the access

and 31. Such an arrangement, however, was probably peculiar to particular
individuals, or to great houses and persons of wealth, for the usual situation
for images of the *Lares* was over or beside the hearth (*focus*) in the great
hall or *atrium* of the house.

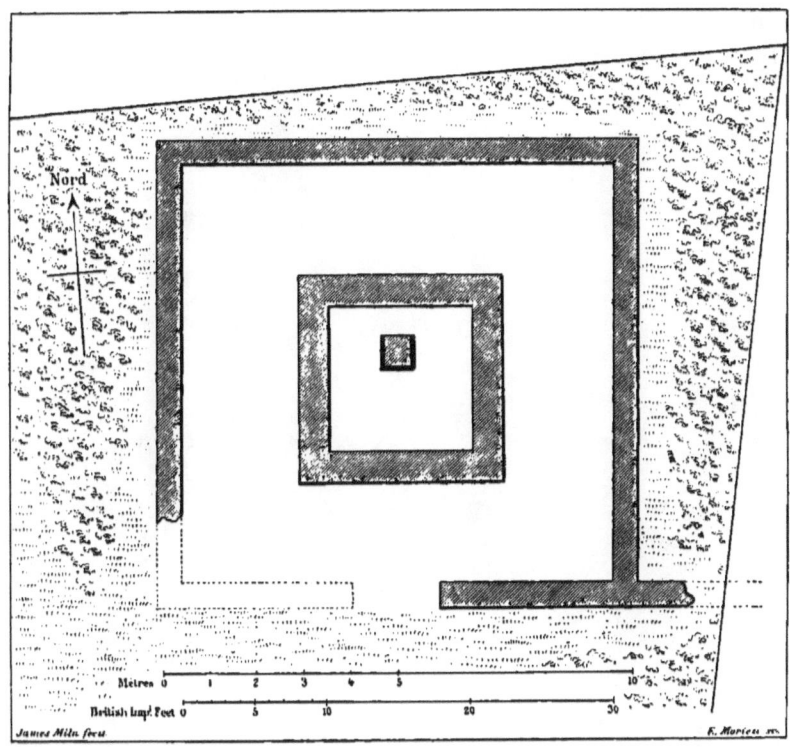

Nord

| Metres 0 | | 1 | 2 | 3 | 4 | 5 | | | | 10 |
| British Imp.¹ Feet 0 | | | 5 | | 10 | | 20 | | | 30 |

James Miln fecit

E. Morieu sc.

To face page 78. D, PLATE I.—PLAN OF THE LARARIUM, MOUND D.

had been by wooden steps, which have long since disappeared, leaving no trace of their existence.

The masonry of this building, constructed in the small cubic stones used by the Romans, was not by any means so carefully finished as those found under the Mounds B and C. It had a much older appearance. The floor was of a hard concrete, formed from argillaceous earth and small water-worn pebbles.

The following objects were found during the excavation of this mound. On the outside of the building, near the entrance, a pair of iron compasses, very much oxidised. (D, pl. II. fig. 1, natural size.)

Several fragments of wall plaster painted blood-red.

Several fragments of pottery, in fine gray paste, well fired, ornamented with a red trellis-work in relief, on a dark ground. (D. pl. II. fig. 2, natural size.)

On the outside of the west wall of the building several fragments of pottery, which served to reconstruct the form of a bowl, in reddish-brown paste, of rude workmanship, and badly fired. (D, pl. II. fig. 3.)

Fragments of statuettes, in white terra-cotta, of the goddess of maternity, and of Venus Anadyomene. (D, pl. IV., V., and VI.)

On the outside of the north wall of the building:

Fragments of coarse pottery, in gray and brownish-black paste, badly fired.

On the outside of the east wall of the building:

Fragments of statuettes, in white terra-cotta, of the goddess of maternity, and of the Venus Anadyomene.

Fragments of a vase, in yellow paste, having a three-lobed mouth. (D, pl. II. fig. 4.)

Several fragments of rude pottery, and bottoms and rims of vases, in gray and brown paste, badly fired.

In clearing out the interior of the building there were found in the passage or *enceinte* on the south side :

A small piece of a marble slab, red, with white veins.

Fragments of vases, in coarse yellowish-red paste.

Part of the handle of a vase, having vertical striæ in relief, separated by lines of little holes which perforate the handle ; paste dark brown. (D, pl. II. fig. 5.)

The upper part of a vase with a wide mouth, having a rude ornament formed on the neck by the prints of the potter's fingers, in coarse paste, and badly fired. (D, pl. III. fig. 1.)

Several fragments of the same kind, with which two similar vases were reconstructed. The smallness of the prints of the potter's fingers on all these vases leads one to suppose that they had been made by women. In the potteries of Malansac and Rieux in Brittany it is the women who make and fire all the varieties of the coarser domestic pottery manufactured in these establishments ; while the work of the men is limited to preparing the paste and modelling the larger and heavier vases, as has been already described. Brogniart, in his *Traité des Arts Ceramiques*, gives a very interesting description of this manufacture.

In the passage on the east side :

Fragments of coarse pottery, and of statuettes in terra-cotta.

The tooth of a bear, hollowed out and perforated with a hole at the half of its length, so as to form a sort of whistle or hunting-call. (D, pl. III. fig. 2, natural size.)

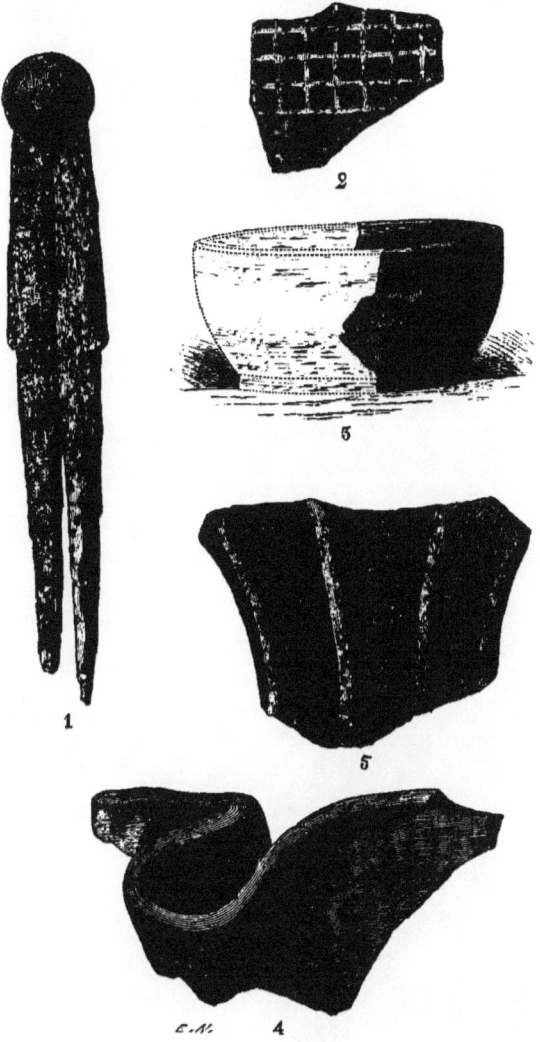

1   2   3   5   4

E. N.

      D, PLATE II.

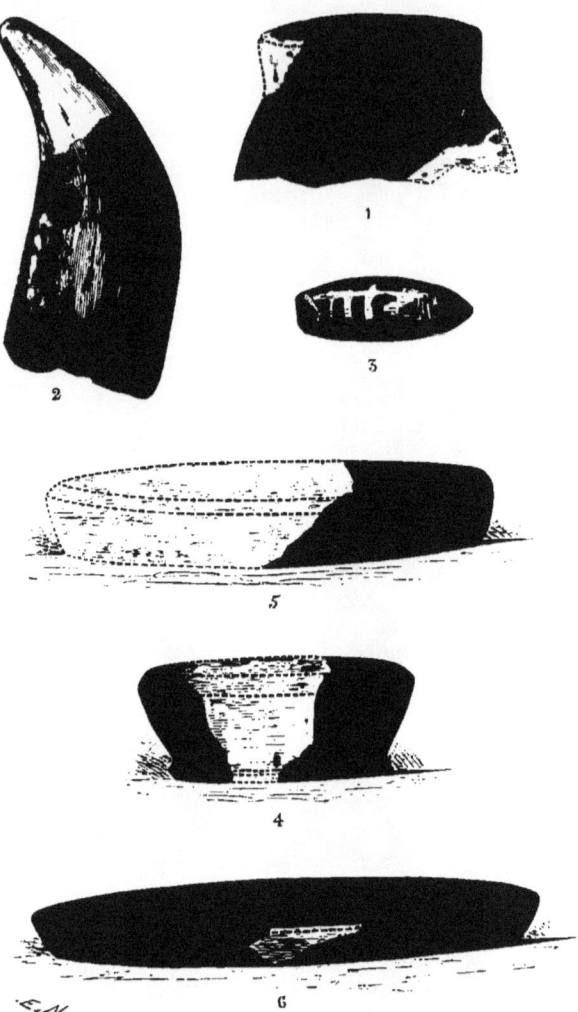

1

2

3

5

4

6

D, PLATE III.

Within the inner square:

The half of a stone axe or hammer, in polished granite, having a hole perforated for the handle.

A necklace bead in black glass, opaque, ornamented with circular bands in white enamel, one of which is undulating. (D, pl. III. fig. 3, natural size.)

A few fragments of thin clear glass.

Fragments of pottery, from which the three following vases were reconstructed :—

A sort of bowl, 6 inches in diameter, $2\frac{1}{2}$ inches deep, in coarse brown paste, badly fired; sides thick and nearly vertical; rim with a bevelled edge. (D, pl. III. fig. 4.)

A flat dish, $9\frac{1}{2}$ inches in diameter, $1\frac{1}{4}$ inch deep, in coarse brown paste, badly fired, and with deep bevelled edges. (D, pl. III. fig. 5.)

A flat dish, diameter $10\frac{1}{2}$ inches, depth $\frac{3}{4}$ inch, in fine blue paste, well fired, of nearly the same form as the preceding

G

vase, but having the sides more spread out.   (D, pl. III.
fig. 6.)

Numerous fragments, in white terra-cotta, of statuettes of
the Venus Anadyomene and of the Goddess of Maternity.

Many of the fragments of statuettes found inside the
building united exactly with those found on the outside, and
thus enabled me in a measure to complete the various
statuettes figured in the accompanying engravings.   (D, pl.
IV. V. and VI., one fourth of the actual size.)

These statuettes are not exactly alike, and although rudely
modelled, are not entirely destitute of artistic feeling.   The
Venus Anadyomene is represented standing on a hemispherical base, the right hand twining the long tresses of
hair, whilst the left holds the drapery.   The goddess of
maternity is represented by a female figure clothed in a
long tunic, seated in a sort of arm-chair formed of wicker
work.   In some figures she is represented suckling one, in
others, two infants.

Similar statuettes, which have been found in many parts
of France, have been described by M. Mazard in his descriptive study of the ceramics of the Museum of Gallo-Roman
Antiquities at St. Germain-en-Laye, as imitations of Greek
and Roman statues.   Other writers speak of them as representing Latona, the protectress of mothers and nurses ;
Lucina, who presided at accouchements ; and also as representing Leda, Juno, and even Isis.   De Caumont states that
sometimes these have been taken for statues of the blessed
Virgin, and that in some places their discovery has been
regarded as miraculous, and has given rise to pilgrimages.*

* _Ere Gallo-romaine_, 2de edition, p. 586.   Par. M. A. de Caumont
Caen, 1870.   F. le Blanc Hardel.

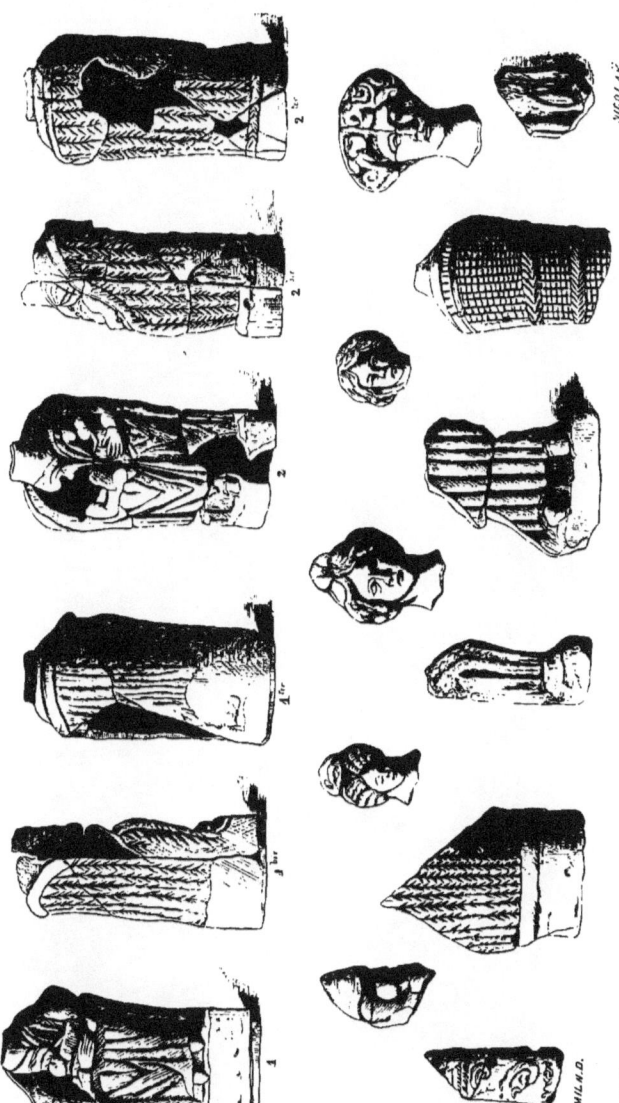

MILN.D.   NICOLAY.

D. PLATE. IV.—STATUETTES OF VENUS GENETRIX.

To face page 82.

II, PLATE V.—STATUETTES OF THE VENUS ANADYOMENE.

To face page 81.

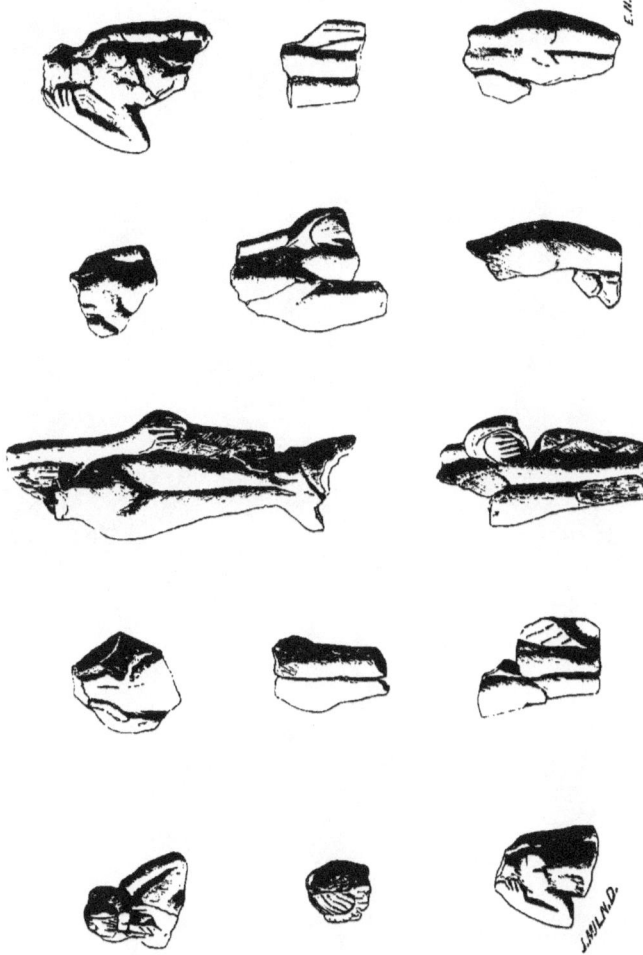

E.H.

J.MILN.D.

To face page 82.

D, PLATE VI.—FRAGMENTS OF STATUETTES OF THE VENUS ANADYOMENE.

The reunion here of so many statuettes representing the same divinity leads me to suppose that the little temple in which they were found had been dedicated to Venus Genetrix.   The pedestal, of which the base was found *in situ*, supported, in all probability, a statue of this goddess, and one may look upon the numerous small statuettes as votive offerings which had been deposited, and of which some had been broken and others carried off, and with these the principal statue, at the time of the pillage and destruction of the Bossenno.

M. Tudot finds a proof that the worship of Venus was general among the Gauls, from the reproach addressed by Saint Augustine to his contemporaries, that they filled a lararium with divinities, amongst whom Venus always presided.*

The pottery found in the Mound D is of a different character from that found in the Mounds A, B, and C.   It is nearly all of primitive forms, badly fired, in a coarse paste, which had a greasy unctuous feeling to the touch.   The weight of the fragments collected was 27 lbs.

The earth we removed from the interior of this building was laid aside and afterwards passed through sieves.   This operation yielded thirteen Roman coins.   This is a much greater number than were found in the Mounds B and C. May we suppose of these, as of the small statuettes, that they had been offerings made to the presiding divinity of the

* Collection de figurines in argile, oeuvres premières de l'art Gauloise, avec les noms des ceramistes qui les ont executées, par Edmond Tudot, p. 270.   Paris : Rollin et Feuardent.

temple? These coins are all in bronze, and embrace a period of 184 years, from the year A.D. 169, the date of the third consulate of Marcus Aurelius, to A.D. 353, the epoch of the death of Magnentius. The following is a detailed description of these coins in chronological order :—

Two of Marcus Aurelius, large brass.

1. M. ANTONINVS. AVG. TR. P. XXIII. (Marcus Antoninus tribunitiæ potestate 23°.) The head laurelled, turned to the right.

Reverse: SALVTI. AVG. COS. III. S. C. (Saluti Augusti consul tertium senatus consulto.) Health, erect, and turned to the left, holds a sceptre and sacrificial cup, in which a serpent drinks. (922, J. C. 169.) (Cohen, 618.)

2. M. ANTONINVS. AVG. TR. P. XXVII. (Marcus Antoninus Augustus tribunitiæ potestate 27.) Bust laurelled and turned to the right.

Reverse: RELIG. AVG.; on the exergue IMP. VI. COS. III.; on the field S. C. (Religio Augusti. Imperator sexto consul tertium, Senatus consulto.) Mercury turned to the left, erect, on a pedestal, holding a caduceus. An exchange in a temple, with four columns and arches. The four columns on the pediment are represented, a turtle, a ram, a caduceus, a cock, a plumed helmet, and a purse. Eckhel explains, according to Diodorus Siculus, the reason why Mercury is represented as the type of religion on the coins of Marcus Aurelius. "In Egypt Mercury was the director of the worship of the gods and of sacrifices." (Cohen, 614; Liv. i., chap. xvi.)

A large brass of Septimius Severus, very much defaced.

Four of Gallienus, small brass.

1. GALLIENVS. AVG. (Gallienus Augustus.)   Bust radiated, turned to the right, with a cuirass.

Reverse: FORTVNA REDVX. (Fortuna redux.) Fortune erect, turned to the left, holding a rudder and cornucopia.

2, 3, 4. GALLIENVS. AVG. (Gallienus Augustus.) Bust radiated, turned to the right, with cuirass.

Reverse: MARTI PACIFERO. (Marti pacifero.) Mars helmeted, erect, turned to the left, holding an olive branch, leaning on a shield; his spear placed on his left arm, in the field A. (Cohen, 354.)

A small brass of Tetricus the elder, much defaced.

Two of Tetricus the younger, small brass, both alike.

C. P. E. TETRICVS. CAES. (Caius Pius Esuvius Tetricus Cæsar.)   Head radiated, turned to the right, with the paludamentum.

Reverse: PIETAS. AVGVSTO. (Pietas Augustorum.) Aspersor, simpulum, sacrificial vase turned to the left, sacrificial knife and divining rod. (Cohen, 32.)

A small brass of Constans I.

D. N. CONSTANS. P. F. AVG. (Dominus noster Constans Pius Felix Augustus.)   Bust, with diadem, turned to the right, with the paludamentum and cuirass.

Reverse: FEL. TEMP. REPARATIO. (Felix temporum reparatio.)   Constans erect, to the left, in military costume, on a vessel going to the left, holding a globe surmounted by a phœnix and imperial standard; to the right, on the vessel, Victory, seated, holds the rudder and regards the emperor. (Cohen, 114.)

G 2

A second brass of Magnentius.

IMP. CAE. MAGNENTIVS AVG.   (Imperator Cæsar
Magnentius Augustus.)   Bust nude, turned to the right,
with the paludamentum.

Reverse : FEL. TEMP. REPARATIO.   (Felix temporum reparatio.)   Magnentius in military costume erect,
turned to the left, on a vessel going to the left, holding a
Victory and the imperial standard.   To the right, on the
vessel, Victory seated holding the rudder.   (Cohen, 35.)

LECH AT PLOUHARNEL.

VI.

EXCAVATIONS IN THE MOUND E.

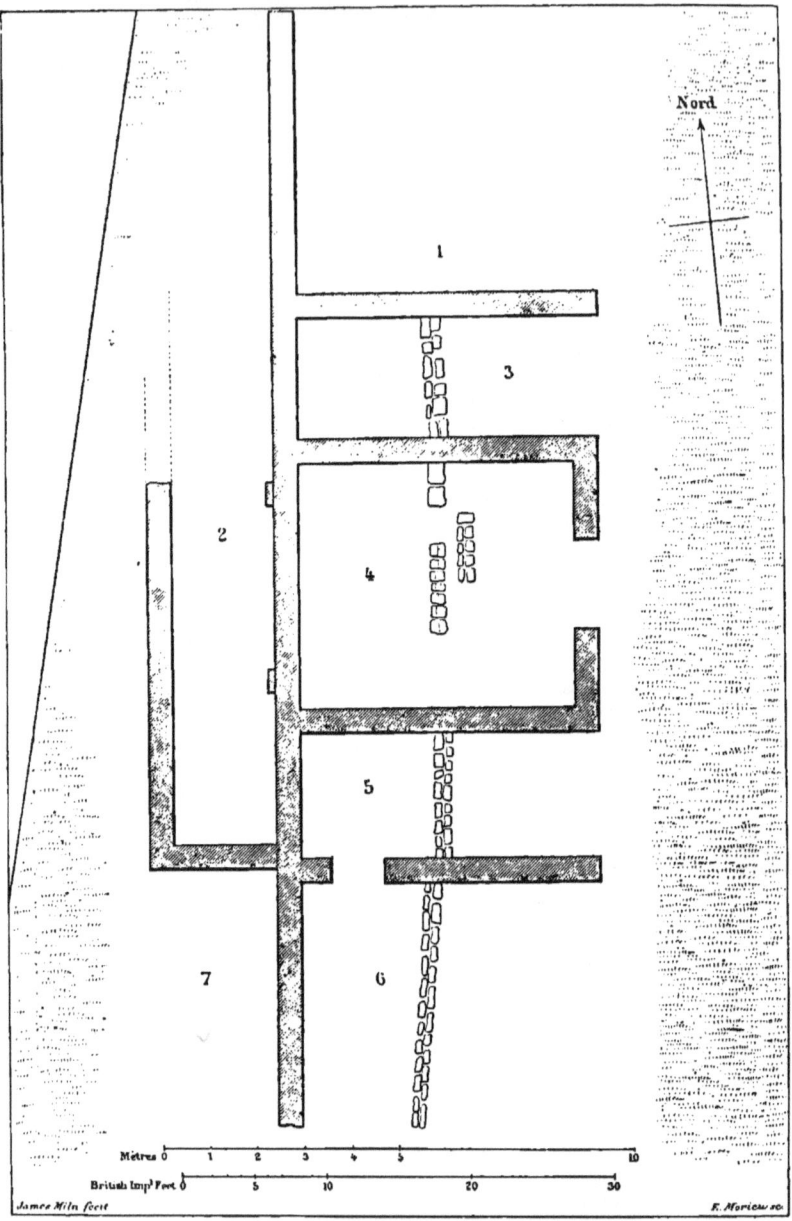

Nord

1

3

2

4

5

7   6

Mètres 0   1   2   3   4   5   10

British Imp¹ Feet 0   5   10   20   30

James Miln fecit

E. Morieu sc.

To face page 89.   E, PLATE I.—PLAN OF THE VILLA AGRARIA.

THE MOUND E.

THE Mound E, of an oblong form, and covered with dwarf trees and bushes, measured 66 feet from north to south, 33 feet from east to west, and had an average height of 6 feet. It was situated to the west of the Mound B, and lay nearly parallel to it. Corn-fields surrounded it on the north, south, and west sides, and a road passed along the east side. The exploration of this mound was commenced on the 23d July 1875.

The remains of the walls of a house were soon exposed, built with the small cubic stones used by the Romans, bound with lime mortar, and having at intervals a layer of large bricks. It soon became evident that these ruins had been encroached upon by the cultivation of the surrounding corn-fields, and by the formation of the road, both of which had destroyed the walls in several places. Afterwards, when the mounds E and F had been excavated, and the buildings found under them exposed to view, we could see that the walls of E, if prolonged to F, would join exactly to the buildings found under that mound. The proprietors of the corn-fields kindly permitted a few holes to be dug after the harvest was over, and in these, at a depth of 3 feet 6 inches, the continuation of the foundations of the wall between E and F were found. In the adjoining field, on the north side of the building, it was found, in a similar way, that the foundations of the walls were also prolonged to the north.

Permission could not be obtained to pursue these researches in a regular way, and this prevents my being able to give either the complete form of the building, or to indicate with certainty the destination of the different apartments. The accompanying ground-plan of the Mound E represents these ruins in the state in which they were when newly excavated, and the following description of the different rooms is given in the order in which they were discovered.

In the room No. 1 the west and south walls alone remained, and of these only four or five courses of masonry. There was neither plaster on the walls nor cement on the floor, which, however, was sufficiently hard and had been formed apparently from beaten earth. The walls were in a bad state of preservation, as were all the other walls of this house. A large quantity of Roman roofing-tiles (*tegulæ* and *imbrices*), for the most part broken in fragments, lay scattered on the floor. There were also to be seen, as in all the buildings hitherto explored, the unmistakable proofs of the fire which had destroyed them.

The division No. 2 extended along the west side of the building, and seemed, judging from a few faint traces on the floor, to have been divided into a number of small rooms. The west wall had only its two lower courses remaining, so that it was impossible to ascertain whether there had been any doors on this side. The east wall had some portions of the plaster which had once covered it still adhering, and the fact that it was not bonded at the corners of the room No. 4 indicated that that room had been constructed before the other parts of the house.

The room No. 3 measured 20 feet 9 inches in length by
8 feet 3 inches in breadth.   Three courses of masonry alone
remained of the north wall.   The south and west walls had an
average height of 3 feet 6 inches, and were in a better state of
preservation.   A few pieces of plaster remained adhering to
the south wall.   No trace of even the foundation of a wall
was found on the east side.   The floor was formed of a
mixture of earth and small water-worn pebbles.   In the middle
of this room the foundation of a wall in large roughly-dressed
stones traversed the apartment in a slightly slanting direction.
The top of these stones was about six inches above the level
of the floor.

The room No. 4 measured 19 feet in length by 17 feet in
breadth.   The average height of what remained of the walls
was 2 feet 9 inches.   It was larger and in a better state of
preservation than any of the other rooms of this building.
A doorway on the east side gave access from the exterior.   The
walls had been covered with plaster, and on the floor, which
was similar to that of the room No. 3, was the continuation of
the foundation of the wall described in connection with that
room.   This foundation was afterwards found to be continued in
the floors of the rooms Nos. 5 and 6.   On the right-hand side
of this foundation, in the room No. 4, was a piece of masonry
of an oblong form, the stones of which were reddened by the
action of fire.   It was covered with cinders, scoriæ, and lumps
of iron, and seemed to be the remains of a furnace or forge.

The room No. 5 measured 20 feet 9 inches in length by
8 feet 3 inches in breadth.   No trace of a wall was found
on the east side; those remaining on the north, south, and
west side had an average height of 3 feet.   A doorway in

the south wall gave access to the room No. 6.   No trace of
plaster was found on the walls nor of cement on the floor.

The dimensions of the room No. 6 could not be ascer-
tained, as it extended under the adjoining field, where I had no
permission to continue the diggings.   The floor was formed
of earth and small rounded water-worn pebbles.

The room No. 7 was under the same conditions as No. 6.
The floor was exceedingly hard.

The following objects were found in working round the
outside, and in clearing out the different rooms of this
building :- -

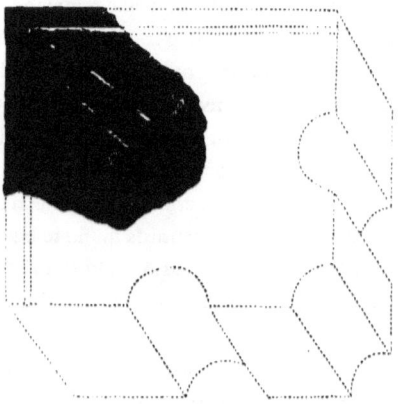

Two fragments of a curious brick, in grayish earth, pierced
with circular holes and having their exterior edges polished
by friction, were found on the east side of the building, at the
foot of the wall of the room No. 4.

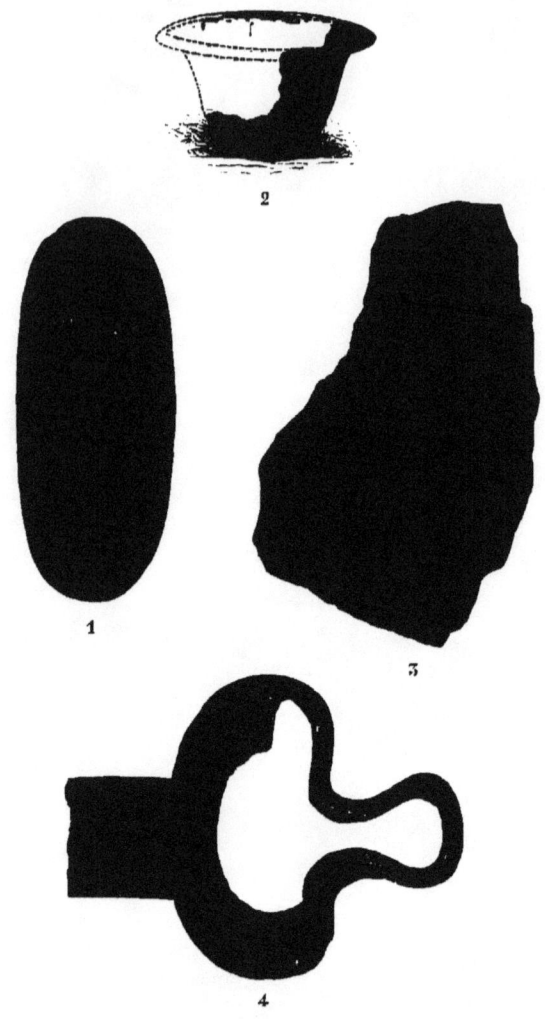

2

1

3

4

To face page 93.   E. PLATE II.

This brick had formed one of a series which admitted of being placed in and withdrawn from the window of an apartment into which the round holes served to circulate light and air.   Two similar bricks were found by M. Parenteau in the diggings at Pouzauges.*

Near these fragments of a brick were the following objects :—

A pestle or rubbing-stone in granite, length $5\frac{1}{2}$ inches. (E, pl. II. fig. 1.)

Part of a small cup, $3\frac{1}{2}$ inches in diameter, in iridescent glass.   (E, pl. II. fig. 2.)

Pieces of an iron sword-blade, very much oxidised.

Iron clamps and nails of different sizes.

In the room No. 1 :

Fragment of a thin bronze plate, 2 inches long, covered with a fine patina, and having two rivets affixed.

Numerous discs formed from brick tiles, similar to those found in the Mounds B and C, varying in diameter from $1\frac{1}{2}$ inch to $3\frac{1}{2}$ inches.

Several fragments of pottery of Celtic type, in coarse

---

* "Grande brique en terre cuite modelée à la main, à base large.   Elle est percée de grands trous disposés régulièrement sur une ligne circulaire ; ses deux faces sont couvertes d'ornements gravés en creux, avec une pointe sèche, avant la cuisson, et faisait partie d'un tout composé de deux briques semblables placées l'une sur l'autre, et dont les trous se raccordaient.   Les dessins offrent la plus grande analogie avec les feuilles de fougères de notre pays, et les guillochures des bracelets gaulois, que l'on rencontre souvent dans nos contrees.   Cette brique a été ramassée par moi sous les ruines du *vicus* de Bournigal, au pied du vieux château de Pouzauges (Vendée), parmi des débris gaulois sans nombre : murs construits en pierres sèches ; fragments de poteries, épées, fers de flèches et poignard en fer."—*Essai sur des Poteries antiques de l'ouest de la France*, par F. Parenteau.   Nantes, 1865.

orange-coloured paste, decorated with close vertical striæ engraved by hand. (E, pl. II. fig. 3, natural size.)

Several fragments of large amphoræ in a yellow paste.

In the room No. 2 :

A large quantity of the bones of ruminants, teeth of the ox and pig, and shells of edible molluscs.

A bodkin in polished bone similar to those found in the Mounds B and C; length 9 inches.

The upper part of a vase, larger diameter 4½ inches, in a grayish-brown paste, having a large trilobed orifice ; the handle, with cords in relief, joins on to the edge of the rim. (E, pl. II. fig. 4.) Vases of this form are to this day manufactured in Brittany : the orifice is obtained by the compression of the anterior part of the neck by the thumb and forefinger.

In the room No. 3 :

Numerous discs formed from tiles, diameter 1½ and 3½ inches.

Several nails and pieces of rod iron, much oxidised.

Several fragments of cups and bottles in white and blue glass.

In the room No. 4 :

A small pestle formed of granite.

Fragment of an ornament cut in rock crystal.

A rounded flint stone like a beach pebble, perforated by a circular hole, in which a bronze ring is inserted. This curious object may probably have been worn as an amulet.

A bronze object, use unknown, but possibly intended to be worn as an ornament. This interesting piece of fine workmanship is formed by flat bands forming an equilateral

E, PLATE III.

triangle, and at the angles, circles and dragons' heads. The base is formed by another band forming a cross with four circles cut open. The whole object is engraved with an ornamentation in lines and points. (E, pl. III. fig. 2, natural size.)

A Roman coin, second brass, re-struck. Part of what appears to have been a tin buckle.

A statuette in bronze was found in the south-east corner of this room which somewhat resembles the small statuettes of the bull Apis exhibited in the Egyptian rooms of the British Museum, and also in the Museum of the Louvre. The chromo-lithograph E, pl. VI., represents this curious object, natural size. It will be further alluded to at the conclusion of this chapter.

A quantity of iron rings, clamps, nails, and pieces of rod iron, were scattered about near the construction which resembled a forge or furnace.

An iron lance or arrow head, having a hollow stem for receiving the shaft, much oxidised. (E, pl. III. fig. 3, natural size.)

A large iron hook, apparently a fishing-hook, much oxidised. (E, pl. III. fig. 4, natural size.)

An iron knife, much oxidised. (E, pl. III. fig. 5, natural size.)

Several pieces of ironwork, which seemed to have been door fastenings.

Neck of a bottle in bluish-coloured glass, and a few fragments, some of fine clear glass, and others of a blue colour.

Several whorls rudely formed of a coarse red paste, having in some cases the holes which perforated them situated near the edge and obliquely inclined; similar to those already alluded to in the Mounds B and C, as having been probably used by fishermen.

Numerous fragments of rudely-formed pottery of Celtic type in a grayish-brown micaceous paste.

In the room No. 5 :

Three pestles or rubbing-stones in granite from 5 to 6 inches in length.

A signet ring in bronze. (E, pl. III. fig. 6, natural size.) This ring contains a setting in blue glass, on which is engraved

the accompanying figure,

Fragments of pottery in a brownish paste, from which a hemispherically-shaped cup was constructed; diameter 6 inches, height 3½ inches, having a collar on the exterior of the rim, and another rim lapping over from the middle part of the vase. (E, pl. IV. fig. 1.)

A bowl, also reconstructed, 7 inches in diameter and 3 inches in height, in a reddish-yellow paste, having a hemispherical base and vertical sides. On the middle part are three collars in relief, the intervals between which are ornamented with diagonal striæ cut hollow. (E, pl. IV. fig. 2.)

Fragment of a vase in red paste, having a vitreous glazing, bearing in relief the figure of the sea-horse. (E, pl. V. fig. 1, natural size.)

Bottom of a vase in red lustrous ware, on which is the potter's mark, represented in the accompanying engraving.

1

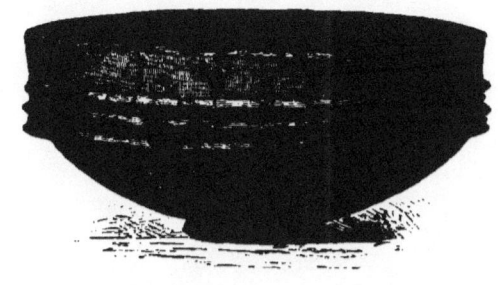

2

E.N.   3

4

To face page 96.   E, PLATE IV.

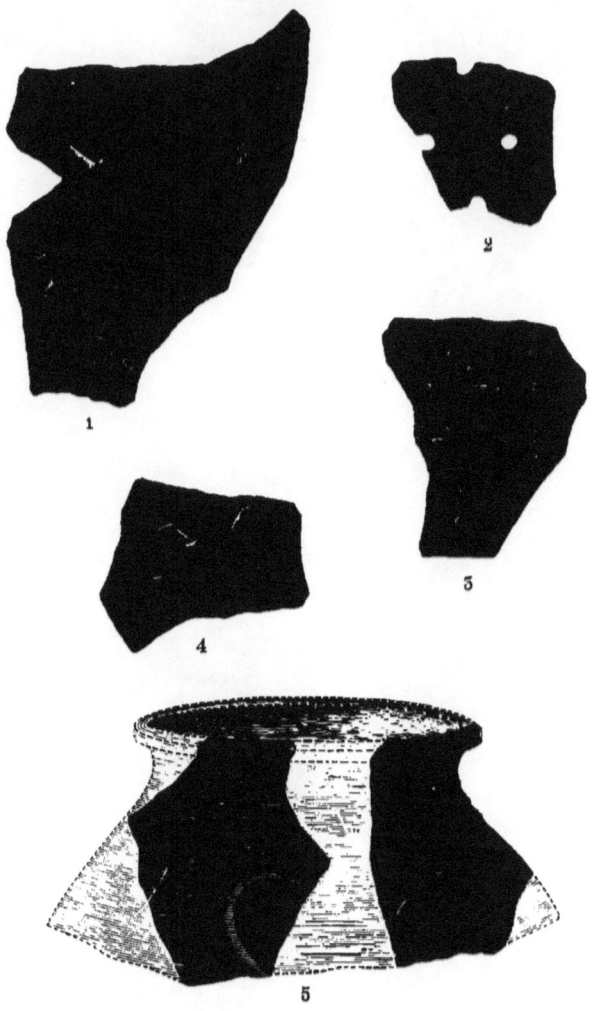

1

2

3

4

5

Fragment of Celtic pottery in brownish-gray paste, ornamented with points and horizontal lines incised. (E, pl. IV. fig. 3, natural size.)

In the room No. 6 :

Several fragments of vases in red lustrous ware of the same kind as those figured in the engraving, B, pl. XIV. fig. 2.

Fragment of a vase in gray paste, pierced with small circular holes which had been made after the firing. (E, pl. V. fig. 2, natural size.)

Fragment of Celtic pottery in brownish-gray paste, ornamented with a large band of juxtaposed undulating lines, incised. (E, pl. IV. fig. 4, natural size.)

In the room No. 7 :

One half of the bottom of a vase in red lustrous ware, bearing part of the potter's stamp.

Several fragments in red lustrous ware, ornamented in relief with garlands and running animals.

Several other fragments, also of Gallo-Roman type, in a fine yellow paste, having a black vitreous glazing, ornamented with figures, etc., in relief, two of which are represented (E, pl. V. figs. 3 and 4, natural size).

Several fragments of a vase of similar type to the two preceding specimens were found at the foot of the wall on the outside of the house, near the entrance of the room No. 4 ;

H

represented for comparison with the others (E, pl. V. fig. 5, natural size).

The fragments of pottery collected in the Mound E weighed 196 lbs. net.

Having now finished the enumeration of the objects found under the Mound E, I may be permitted to revert to the statuette of an ox in bronze (E, pl. VI.) found in the room No. 4, and as having some connection therewith to narrate some customs still observed at Carnac, which would appear to have been handed down from a very remote epoch.

When the statuette was found in the corner of the room, the workmen all crowded round it in a state of excitement, and exclaimed, " Here is a discovery ; we have found the ox of St. Carnely."

This requires an explanation. The patron Saint of the parish of Carnac is Saint Cornelius, the protector of bestial, who is supposed to have been pope during the third century.

In the Breton dialect of Carnac his name is pronounced Carnély.

The great fête of the year at Carnac is the anniversary of Saint Carnely, which takes place at the autumnal equinox. A pilgrimage, or as it is named in Brittany, the pardon of St. Carnely, is then held, and goes on for a week. Numerous services are held in the church, and processions march from the church with banners flying to the fountain of St. Carnely (E, pl. VII.), and thence round the village. A fair is held in a field adjoining the village for the sale of bestial ; the streets are lined with booths, shows, merry-go-rounds, and the usual accompaniments of a country fair. Numerous pilgrims resort to this from all parts of Brittany, clad in the costumes of their respective districts ; they come to implore the protection of Saint Carnely for their bestial.

J. MAIR. sc.

To face page 98.

E., PLATE VI.—STATUETTE OF OX IN BRONZE.

FOUND IN THE CENTRAL CHAMBER OF THE VILLA AGRARIA IN THE MOUND E (ACTUAL SIZE).

On arriving at Carnac they at once enter the church and kneel down before a gilded bust containing the relics of Saint Carnely ; thence they proceed to the outside, where a numerous band of mendicants assail them with cries and lamentations for alms.   These are granted sometimes on the conditions that the recipient makes the round of the church on his knees. The pilgrims then proceed slowly, solemnly, and in silence, round the outside of the church.   They kneel down before a statue of Saint Carnely, supported by two oxen, placed above the west door, and repeat inwardly a prayer; thence they proceed in the same solemn manner to the fountain of Saint Carnely, which is situated about 200 yards to the west of the church.   Here numerous boys belonging to the village, for the remuneration of a few sous, present them with bowls of water freshly drawn from the fountain.   The pilgrims kneel down before the fountain, taste the water, wet their face and hands, and then elevating their hands towards heaven, allow the water to trickle down their arms.

When this ceremony is finished they return in the same solemn manner to the church; there they deposit their offer-ing in the box placed alongside of the gilded bust of the saint; should the donation, however, happen to be of a considerable amount, it is placed in the hands of the church-warden, and the amount is named from the pulpit on the following Sunday.

Another curious ceremony, also having reference to the health of their bestial, is sometimes performed by the peasants in the neighbourhood of Carnac.   It is called the nocturnal procession, and is performed generally near midnight.

So soon as the cure of sick animals has been effected, the proprietors arrange for a nocturnal procession.

On the following night all the bestial of the homestead

H 1

are assembled, and the procession marches solemnly, and in strict silence to Carnac. A halt is made before the north door of the church, where the conductors kneel down and repeat inwardly a prayer; thence they proceed round the church, halting at the west door, and then go on to the fountain of St. Carnely. The conductors again kneel down for a few minutes, then draw water from the fountain, and pour a little over each of the animals. This ceremony over, the procession returns to the north door of the church, and thence always in strict silence to their homes.

Another curious custom always observed in Carnac and the neighbouring communes at the summer solstice, and in which also the bestial are made to perform a part, is the lighting up of bonfires in the evening, after sunset. This is called in the Breton of Carnac *tan heol* (the fire of the sun), and also *tan Sant Jan* (the fire of Saint John).

The young people of Carnac go from house to house during the day, receiving contributions of faggots of wood and bundles of furze, which they transport to the summit of the tumulus or cairn which tops the Mont St. Michel. Towards sunset numerous spectators proceed there, nearly all of whom assist in preparing the bonfire.

Just as the sun sets long clouds of smoke are seen rolling along the ground from the neighbourhood of adjoining farms. If you ask the cause of all this, you are told that these are fires prepared expressly for the cattle, with green broom and fern, so as to produce a dense smoke. In fact it is at this time that the cattle are brought home, and before being housed for the night are made to pass across these fires, the doing of which is supposed to preserve them from all maladies for a year to come.

But let us return to the preparation of the bonfire. It has

To face page 200.

E. PLATE VII.—THE FOUNTAIN OF SAINT CARNELY.

increased in size rapidly, many willing hands lending assistance, and is at length finished ; before lighting, however, we must wait until the fires of the surrounding country have shone out. These soon begin to shoot out from every direction, at Quiberon, Plouharnel, Erdeven, Ploemel, Crach, Locmariaker Arzon, St. Gildas de Rhuis, in the islands of Houat, Hedic, and Belle Isle,—everywhere, as far as the eye can reach, is one immense illumination.

The proper moment for lighting the fire of the Mont St. Michel has arrived ; when it is desired to honour a stranger, he is asked to set fire to the huge pile of furze, which, blazing up in an instant, lightens up the whole hill and neighbourhood, amidst shouts of joy from the spectators.

CROSS ON THE MONT ST MICHEL.

H 2

VII.

EXCAVATIONS IN THE MOUND F.

H 3

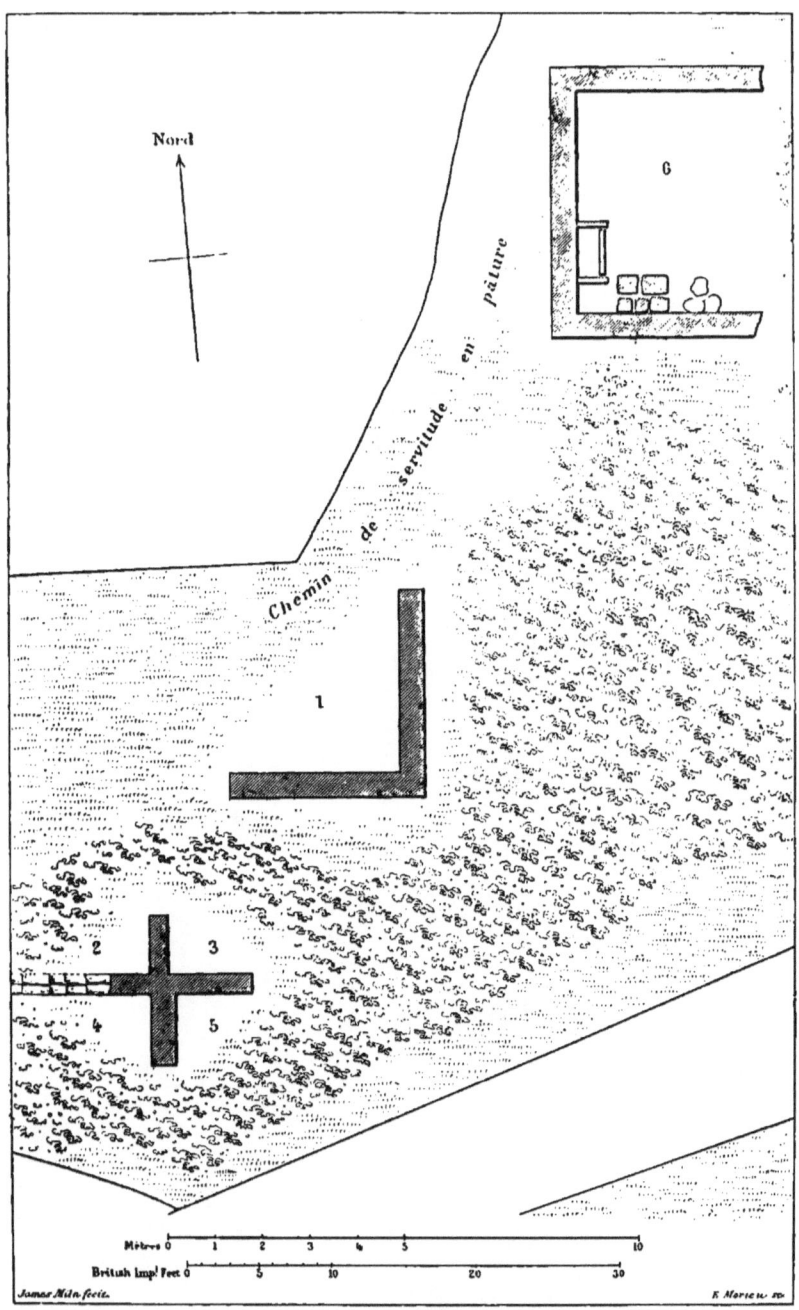

Nord

Chemin de servitude en pâture

G

1

2 3

4 5

Mètres 0 1 2 3 4 5 10

British Impl Feet 0 5 10 20 30

James Milne fecit.

F. Morieu sc.

To face page 105. F, PLATE I.—PLAN OF THE BUILDINGS IN THE MOUND F.

THE MOUND F.

THE exploration of the Mound F was begun on the 10th of August 1875. It consisted of several irregular heaps of earth covered with furze and brambles, bounded on the north by the road already mentioned in the diggings of the Mound E, and on the south by the ancient road leading from Carnac to the Trinité sur Mer. The widening and repairing of these two roads, and the extension of the cultivated fields on the east side of the Mound, have so cut in upon the ruins which my diggings have exposed to view, that very little is left to give an idea of their original construction.

The ancient road just mentioned was widened and repaired when the Duke of Nemours passed this way in 1842. Whilst the work was being done, there were discovered, at the place where it passes close to the Mound F, remains of walls built in small cubic stones bound with mortar, Roman roofing-tiles, and numerous fragments of pottery.

It was not until 1849 and 1850 that the new road between Carnac and the Trinité sur Mer was made. When this was being executed, there were discovered, near where it passes the Bossenno and about 300 yards to the north, several Roman coins, one of which was in gold, having on one side the figure of a horse, on the other the effigy of Caligula. Close to these were found remains of constructions in small cubic stones,

Roman bricks and tiles, and numerous fragments of different kinds of pottery. These discoveries gave rise to a good deal of discussion at the time they were made, but nothing was done to follow up such sure indications, and they were soon forgotten. It was only after the diggings of the Mound F were commenced that I first heard of, and subsequently verified, the above statements.

The ground-plan of the Mound F shows the state of the buildings when the diggings were completed. The walls of these buildings were all constructed with small cubic stones bonded with lime, with the exception of the wall between No. 2 and No. 4, which appeared to be a continuation of the southern *enceinte*, and was built of large irregularly-shaped stones bound with a mortar formed of mud or argillaceous earth.

The building No. 6 was first excavated. There could be little doubt as to its having been used as a blacksmith's workshop, for a construction measuring 4 feet in length, 2 feet 10 inches in breadth, and 1 foot 10 inches in height, which appeared to have been the forge, was built in large dressed stones against the south wall. The upper surface was wasted and reddened in the part which had been occupied as the fireplace, and was covered with lumps of iron, scoriæ, ashes, and pieces of charcoal. A bar of iron one inch in breadth and half an inch in depth was cemented with lead into the west side of this construction just above the lower course of masonry. It projected for twelve inches, and terminated in a bend extending for two inches at right angles. Close to the forge was the water-trough. It was constructed against the west wall with slabs of granite bound at the corners with a rose-coloured cement.

The floors of all the buildings found under the Mound F

1

2

3

4

6

E.N.

5

To face page 107.

F. PLATE II.

were formed of a sort of concrete, and, with the exception of
No. 5, were covered with fragments of roofing-tiles, charcoal,
ashes, and the *debris* which had fallen on them at the period
when they had been burnt. As no other feature worth
mentioning was observed in the buildings Nos. 1, 2, 3, 4, 5, I
shall now proceed with the enumeration of the different objects
found in excavating the Mound F.

In the building No. 1 :
Several fragments of common pottery in gray and in black
paste.

A fine polished stone axe in chloro-melanite * was discovered in the angle formed by the two walls. This fine
specimen was unfortunately much injured by the blow of the
workman's pick : what remains of it measures 5 inches in
length by 2½ inches in breadth.

In the building No. 2 :
A solid bronze ring perforated with a circular hole. (F,
pl. II. fig. 1, natural size.)

Fragment of a small object in bronze, having an ornamentation of circles and points engraved. (F, pl. II. fig. 2,
natural size.)

Fragment of a very thin bronze plate perforated with small
circular holes. (F, pl. II. fig. 3, natural size.)

Several other smaller fragments of the same description,

---

* Chloro-melanite approaches to jadeite in its hard, dense, and fusible
properties. It is a dark green mineral, which at first sight appears black,
but when the thin edge of a fracture is exposed to strong light, is trans-
parent and green. It may therefore be considered as a variety of jadeite, in
which a certain proportion of alumina is replaced by oxide of iron.—
Damour.

and another fragment plated in silver. A stem of iron with a round bronze head; this seemed to have formed part of the handle of a dagger.

A small bronze coin of Claudius the Second, in a bad state of preservation.

Two small bronze coins, illegible.

Fragments of a vase in fine black paste, having a vitreous lustre, large mouth, a collar on the exterior of the rim; badly fired, very fragile. The glazing dissolves on being washed. Length 6 inches. (F, pl. II. fig. 4.)

Handle of a vase in red paste, the ornamentation formed by twisting, similar to that figured (B, pl. VIII. fig. 3).

Rims of terrines in a fine red paste.

The neck of a large amphora in yellow paste.

Part of the handle of a similar amphora.

Bottom of a vase in red lustrous ware termed Samian, ornamented with a herring-bone pattern in relief, obtained from moulds.

Several fragments of the same kind of pottery ornamented with garlands, running animals, and the leaves of aquatic plants in relief, obtained by moulding.

Several fragments which served to reconstruct the greater part of a bowl, diameter 9 inches, height 3 inches, in a dull red paste, rudely ornamented with irregular zones formed of coarsely punctulated lines. (F, pl. II. fig. 5.)

Two small cups measuring $4\frac{1}{4}$ inches in diameter by $2\frac{1}{2}$ inches in height were also reconstructed from fragments of red lustrous ware.

Four dishes measuring from 6 inches to 8 inches in diameter, in a grayish-brown paste, were also reconstructed from fragments. These had been common culinary vessels, similar to that figured (A, pl. III. fig. 5.)

In the building No. 3 :

Some coarse fragments of common pottery of Celtic type in a gray paste badly fired :

In the building No. 4 :

An iron bullock shoe very much oxidised, having three square-headed nails in each side.   It is here figured, full size.

The bones of oxen found in the other Mounds have been recognised by Professor Paul Gervais as those of a small race.   This shoe has also been that of a small animal.   The bovine race to this day in Brittany are, as is well known, celebrated for their small and fine proportions.   We have then in this shoe and in the bones alluded to, an indication that there has been no great change in the size of the Breton oxen since the Roman occupation.

Several iron nails of different sizes, very much oxidised.

Numerous fragments of common Celtic and Gallo-Roman pottery, consisting of bottoms, sides, and rims of culinary vessels.

In the building No. 5 :

An amber bead nearly opaque, diameter $1\frac{1}{4}$ inch, perforated with a circular hole.

Several fragments of common pottery in a micaceous grayish-brown paste.

In the building No. 6 :

Numerous objects in iron were found scattered about the floor. These were of different forms, round, flat, and concave, but all so much oxidised that, notwithstanding every precaution, they could not be extracted from the earth without crumbling into small pieces.

Numerous nails and pieces of rod iron of different sizes, very much oxidised.

Numerous fragments of coarse pottery of Celtic type, in a greyish-brown paste, badly fired.

Several fragments of vases in a brown paste, ornamented with black vitreous bands.

Several fragments of vases, in a yellow paste, ornamented with undulating lines similar to those figured (B, pl. VIII. figs. 4 and 5).

Several fragments served to reconstruct a vase $7\frac{1}{2}$ inches in diameter, in fine black paste, with a vitreous glazing similar to that figured (B, pl. VIII. fig. 2).

The bottom of a large bowl in red lustrous ware, ornamented with parallel zones of lozenge-shaped figures, stamped with a herring-bone pattern. The length of this fragment is 7 inches. (F, pl. II. fig. 6.)

Several fragments of red lustrous ware, ornamented with garlands, figures of running animals, and leaves of aquatic plants.

Other fragments of red lustrous ware served to reconstruct a vase 7½ inches in diameter, having a rim slanting over from the middle part, the same as that figured (B, pl. XIV. fig. 2).

The fragments of pottery collected in the Mound F weighed 99 lbs. nett.

CROSS AT COET-A-TOUS.

VIII.

EXCAVATIONS IN THE MOUND G.

THE MOUND G.

A VERY small mound, topped by an old hawthorn tree, was situated in the southern *enceinte*, at a distance of 28 yards from the ancient road which traverses the Bossenno. It is marked on the general plan of the Bossenno by the letter G.

In cutting a wide trench from north to south across this mound, we came upon numerous small cubic building stones, large dressed stones, portions of overturned walls, fragments of roofing-tiles (*tegulæ* and *imbrices*), and the *debris* of a building which had evidently been completely destroyed. Here also, as in all the mounds hitherto explored, were the evidences of a violent conflagration, viz. ashes, charcoal, and granite stones vitrified.

The following objects were collected during the cutting of the trench, viz.—

Several pieces of window-glass of a greenish colour, polished on one face and rough on the other, similar to those found in the Mound C (the baths).

Fragments of a glass bottle of square form, thick, and of a bluish colour.

A few fragments of fine pottery in a fine black paste, with vitreous glazing, tender and badly fired.

Numerous fragments of common gray pottery.

Handle and part of the body of a vase in yellow paste,

well fired, decorated with diagonal bands, and between these
numerous circles, irregularly placed, obtained by stamping.
A vase measuring 6 inches in diameter and 3 inches in height,
identically similar to this fragment, was found in the excavations of the Gallo-Roman constructions of Jublains and is
now exhibited in the museum at Mayenne. It is figured in
the accompanying engraving.

As no remains of any construction worth following could
be found, we filled up the trench and abandoned the Mound G.

Two other trenches were next cut across the *enceinte* at
different points between the Mounds F and G, which yielded
similar results.

Up to this time we had explored seven mounds, in doing
which the ruins of the dwellings of people of a former age had
been exposed to view, and numerous objects collected, all
tending to throw some light on their mode of life and occupation. It had frequently occurred to me, not only when
examining these ruins, but also the indications of others which
extended far on every side, that the population must have

been of considerable extent, and that some evidence as to their mode of sepulture ought to be found in the vicinity.

The researches made of late years by the Polymathic Society of the Morbihan have proved that the dolmens of that country had been places of sepulture, in some of which cremation, in others inhumation, had been used. The age of these monuments, however, is still a mystery, although recent discoveries show that some of them had been used as places of sepulture in the third century.

The discovery made of late years of cinerary vases, ashes and charcoal, under a few of the menhirs, tends to show that these had been funeral monuments, whilst it does not prevent others from having a different signification.

Cæsar, who was not only a great captain* but an able writer, mentions that the funerals in Gaul were magnificent for that country, that the body of the defunct was burnt with everything that he had most cherished, even his animals, and formerly his slaves and freedmen.† The Commentaries, however, preceded the date of the ruins of the Bossenno by four centuries, judging from the evidence of the coins found there. Time enough had elapsed for many changes to have taken place in the manners and customs of a people.

The following researches were made with a view of obtaining some information on the mode of sepulture which had been practised by the inhabitants of the Bossenno.

---

* Tacitus, who wrote of Cæsar *Summus auctorum divus Julius,* differs from him, nevertheless, in many particulars, particularly so as to the funeral rites. The discrepancy may perhaps be accounted for by changes having occurred during the time which separates these authors. Tacitus wrote about the end of the first or beginning of the second century, fully a hundred years after the time when Cæsar wrote the Commentaries.

† Cæsar's Commentaries, 6 lib.

On the west side of the Mound G was the commencement of a row of very small menhirs which extended to the westward from where the traces of the *enceinte* stop. At first sight they appeared to have been large stones which had been cleared away from the neighbouring fields and placed on the low earthen wall which separates the fields 937 Er Prat (the meadow), and 938 Narlier. But how came it that the greater portion were sunk in the earth so as to stand in an upright position? No peasant farmer would have done this, when the laying them lengthways would have answered his purpose so much better.

A trench was cut along the south side of these menhirs: from this we worked round and underneath those still left standing. We found that they had been carefully built round with stones, so as to maintain them in an erect position. In digging round these menhirs we collected several pieces of charcoal, fragments of coarse pottery of a Celtic type in gray and in black paste, several pieces of roofing-tiles (*tegulæ*), and from right underneath the menhirs fragments of vases in red lustrous ware called Samian.

Seeing that nothing more could be done here, we redressed the menhirs which we had overturned, filled up our trenches, and proceeded to the north side of the Bossenno.

The remains of a ruined dolmen were situated on an eminence in the field 639 Er Roch (the rock), about 150 yards to the north of the Mound C (the baths). We commenced excavations both on the inside and on the outside of the ruins, and soon found a few pieces of charcoal and common gray pottery. These, however, were discarded as of no value, when I learned that the fire of Saint John was made here at midsummer; and as this dolmen had evidently been previously ransacked, we renounced farther work here and

Mètres 0   0.50   1   2   3

British Imp¹. Feet 0   1   2   3   4   5   6   7   8

To face page 119.   G, PLATE I.—LARGE MENHIR NEAR THE BOSSENNO.

proceeded westward to examine a large menhir in the vicinity.

This menhir measured 17 feet in length, of which 13 were above ground. It stood in the middle of a field (see the general plan of the Bossenno, No. 619 Er Menhir—the menhir), 200 yards west from the ruined dolmen, which it is supposed by some antiquaries to indicate.

We commenced digging on two sides of the menhir in the field No. 619, and soon found that it was built round with dry stones. These, however, had failed to keep it upright, for it was so much off the perpendicular that I was afraid to continue the diggings all round it. Underneath the menhir was a bed of rich black earth 12 inches in depth ; below this was the primitive rock. Amongst the stones which served to prop up the menhir we found the bottom of a vase, in the fine red ware usually called Samian,* the glazing of which was destroyed ; a rough piece of unworked marble, red, veined

---

*'A few years ago, M. the Abbé du Marc'hallach, Vicar-General to the Bishop of Quimper, executed some researches at the foot of a large menhir, forming part of an alignment of menhirs situated a few miles from that city, in the parish of Ploumelin. Underneath this enormous stone he discovered a Roman coin (middle brass) and several fragments of Roman roofing-tiles (*tegulæ*).

In 1871, M. the Abbé Collet, vicaire of Ploemel, had some diggings made in the tumulus of Mané Ploerig, situated to the north of Han Hon, in the parish of Carnac. He discovered in these diggings two iron lance-heads, an iron ring, two flint arrow-heads, a piece of clear glass, several fragments of roofing-tiles (*tegulæ*), a large quantity of fragments of pottery of different kinds, including a large portion of a fine vase in red lustrous ware (called Samian), ornamented with flowers and garlands in relief. He also found fragments of Roman roofing-tiles in the tumulus of Mané Botgade, situated to the west of Ploemel ; and in the tumulus of Mané Bihuic, situated to the east of Ploemel. I am indebted for these facts to M. the Abbé du Marc'-hallach, and to M. the Abbé Collet.

with white ; a worked flake of dark flint, and several fragments of roofing-tiles (*tegulæ*).

I confine myself for the present to giving the above statements, which I have verified *de visu*, without attempting to
draw any deduction therefrom.   It would require a number
of analogous facts, constituted by careful observers, to enable
one to hazard a conjecture on this association of objects and
monuments of such different origin.

In the neighbourhood of Carnac, where there are so many
dolmens, a sharp-pointed menhir is generally situated either
on the top of the tumulus surmounting the dolmen or in its
immediate vicinity.   The menhirs at the end of the great
alignments are also of a pointed form, and are supposed to
mark the rising and setting of the sun, in some at the solstices,
and in others at the equinoxes, to an observer situated within
the alignments.   After having spent some time in making drawings of the different alignments, one becomes convinced that
the forms of the menhirs are comprised in a few varieties,
which are continually recurring, viz. pointed or needle-shaped
stones, square blocks, long slabs, with their upper edge forming an obtuse angle, pear-shaped monoliths set on their
narrow ends.

In the previous portion of this chapter the Gallo-Roman
antiquities of Jublains have been alluded to ; and as these
highly-interesting remains are not so generally known as they
ought to be, perhaps the following notice may serve to draw
the attention of archæologists towards them, or induce the
tourist to visit what will amply repay the slight deviation he
will have to make from the ordinary railway route between
Paris and Rennes.

The village of Jublains has a population of 1846 inhabitants, and is situated between Mayenne and Evron, in the

department of Mayenne. At the time when Cæsar's legions invaded the country Jublains was a place of some importance —*Næodunum*, the capital of the *Aulerces Diablintes*. Under the Roman civilisation the Gaulish town became a Roman one of some splendour, having its *castra stativa*, temples, theatre, forum, aqueducts, baths, and having roads communicating with Tours, Angers, the valley of Mayenne, Rennes, and Corseul. This Gallo-Roman town was destroyed about the beginning of the fifth century, and, like the Bossenno, was forgotten until the excavations of the last few years brought its remains to light.

CROSS AT HAN HON.

IX.

EXCAVATIONS IN THE MOUND H.

Nord

James Milne fecit.

· To face Page 175.

Metres 0   1   2   3   4   5   6   7   8   9   10

British Imp.Feet 0   5   10   20   30

H, PLATE I.—PLAN OF THE BUILDINGS UNDER THE MOUND H.

E. Morgan & Co.

THE MOUND H.

On the wall which has already been alluded to in the introduction as the northern *enceinte* there was, at a distance of
230 feet west from the Mound D (the temple), another mound,
marked in the plan of the Bossenno by the letter H.

This Mound was of an elliptical form, measured 83 feet
in length, 20 feet in breadth, and 4 feet 6 inches in height.
The height seemed to be partly due to the stones and rubbish
gathered on the adjoining fields having been thrown on it.

On the 17th August 1876 we commenced the excavation
of this mound by opening up the east side, and soon exposed
the large dry stone wall of the *enceinte*. A few feet to the
eastward it stopped short, with its end squared off; then an
interruption for 11 feet, when it again recommenced. This
break in the wall was observed on the ground by the difference of level before the commencement of the diggings. It
appeared to me to have been one of the entrances or ports to
the houses situated within the *enceinte*, which could be easily
barricaded. (See the plan of the Mound H, pl. I.)

Leaving the entrance we again commenced on the east end
of the mound, working to the westward along the wall of the
enceinte. We soon came upon a wall 2 feet 4 inches in breadth,
built in small cubic stones bound with lime mortar, running
parallel to the *enceinte* on the south side, at a distance from it

of 2 feet. At the foot of the eastern end of this wall was a remnant of pavement formed of square tiles. This wall continued for 8 feet; at that distance it was traversed at a right angle by another wall of the same description, but of which the south portion had been destroyed by the cultivation of the adjoining field.

Working round the transverse wall, we came upon another of the same description running parallel to, but situated 2 feet farther from the *enceinte*, so as to form a second narrow passage. We followed this wall to the west, and came on its south side upon another, also of the same description, and forming another narrow passage 3 feet in width. A doorway was found in this last wall, near its western extremity, where the cultivation of the adjoining field had destroyed it. An examination of the plan of the Mound H will convey a better idea of the position of these walls than can be given by any description.

In excavating this mound we found that it was composed for the most part of large unshapely stones. A little below the surface, on the top of the mound, we came upon the upper half of a stone axe in polished diorite.

The following objects were found lower down, on the floor of the passages.

A bronze coin, illegible.

Part of a bronze buckle. (H, pl. II. fig. 3, natural size.)

Portion of a bronze clasp inlaid with silver. (H, pl. II. fig. 1, natural size.)

Several iron nails, much oxidised.

A small ingot of lead.

Two fragments of cups in fine thin glass, the rim turned slightly outwards.

1

2

3

4

5

6

H, PLATE II.

Fragment of a cup in fine thin glass, with straight rim, and having ribbed cannelures in the middle.

Fragment of clear glass with incised ornaments.

A granite stone, measuring 4 inches in length, and weighing 2 lbs. 2 oz. The form reminds one of the plummet used by carpenters and masons. At first sight it seemed to be a weight, but the weight of the Roman pound (6144 grains) does not bear out that idea. It may possibly have served as a sinker for large fishing nets (*sagenæ*). (H, pl. II. fig. 2.)

A sharpening stone or hone, 4 inches in length, much abraded by use.

An unfinished spindle whorl, 2 inches in diameter, in a paste of coarse brick earth, nearly half pierced through on each face.

Several fragments of red lustrous ware, without ornament, from which a vase, 5 inches in diameter, was reconstructed. It is figured in H, pl. II. fig. 5.

Several fragments of a vase, in a fine black paste, with a vitreous glazing, and having straight rim slightly turned outwards; diameter 6½ inches. (H, pl. II. fig. 4.)

Several fragments which gave the form of a dish, in a grayish paste, the sides spreading slightly outwards, and the rim bevelled off to the outside; diameter 8 inches. (H, pl. II. fig. 6.)

Several fragments of red lustrous ware, some of which were plain, others ornamented with leaves of aquatic plants and figures of the *Equus marinus* on the middle part, with flutings superposed; the same as the fragments found in the mounds previously described.

Fragments of large vessels having a spout on the rim, in a yellow paste.

Handles of amphoræ, in a yellow paste.

Neck and handle of a bottle, in yellow paste.

Fragments of different vases, in fine black paste, with vitreous glazing; plain.

Other fragments in black paste, ornamented with zones formed of points incised.

Several bottoms and other fragments of vases, in gray paste and red paste; plain. Other fragments in gray paste, ornamented with vertical and diagonal striæ.

The weight of the pottery collected in this mound amounted to 28 lbs. nett.

DOOR AT KERGOUELLARD.

X.

SUMMARY AND CONCLUSIONS.

K

SUMMARY AND CONCLUSIONS.

HAVING described in the previous chapters the results of the excavations in the Mounds of the Bossenno, I now proceed to draw conclusions from them in regard to the age and character of the buildings, the condition and modes of life of their occupants, and the probable date of the final destruction of the settlement.

It will be sufficiently obvious, from the details already given, that in these buildings we have the remains of a Gallo-Roman establishment. The evidence of this is found in the construction of the walls with small cubic stones regulated at intervals with layers of long bricks, in the roofing-tiles, in the Gallo-Roman pottery, and in the Roman coins.

The excavation of the Mound A disclosed a small dwelling divided into four apartments. In these were found objects of bronze, iron, and glass, pottery, and food refuse, all of which indicated a high degree of civilisation and prosperity.

The removal of the Mound B disclosed a house of eleven apartments, carefully constructed; its walls plastered and decorated. In its rooms were pottery of remarkable fineness, objects of bronze and iron, fine glass ware, Roman coins, and food refuse, all of which indicated a greater amount of wealth and luxury than was implied in the contents of the Mound A.

Under the Mound C there was disclosed a building, forming a dependance of that in the Mound B, carefully constructed, the walls plastered, and richly decorated with painting and curious shell frescoes. It also yielded articles of bronze and iron, glass, pottery, Roman coins, and food refuse.

In the Mound D there appeared another dependance of the Mound B,—a small square construction surrounding another of the same form, in the floor of which was a slab, which seemed to be the base of an altar. Its contents differed widely from those in the other buildings, not only in the absence of food refuse, but in the presence of numerous statuettes of the Venus Anadyomene and the Venus Genetrix, Roman coins, and peculiar pottery.

The Mound E contained a building, of which only seven compartments were determined, less carefully built than those in the Mound B. It was distinguished from the others by the absence of decoration on the walls, and the presence of a statuette and other objects in bronze, articles of iron, pottery, glass, and food refuse.

Under the Mound F was a construction consisting of several buildings, part of which appeared to be a continuation of those under the Mound E, but including a separate one, in which were a forge, a stone trough, scoriæ, and remains of iron implements and pottery.

The Mounds G and H yielded traces of buildings, with objects in bronze and iron, and pottery.

The following quotations from authors who are regarded as authorities on the Gallo-Roman epoch may assist us in deducing conclusions as to the destination of some of these buildings.

De Caumont speaks of certain *villæ* as being so large as to be more like camps than country-houses, and states * "that the finest of the Roman country houses had only one storey ; in other respects they did not differ from the houses in the cities. The greater part of the *villæ* were not only residences for pleasure, but also included what was requisite for the pursuit of agriculture, whether as houses for the cultivators of the soil, for the bestial, or for storing the harvest."

"Columella points out three divisions in the country house which had its farm attached, and the greater part of the Gallo-Roman *villæ* would come under that category. These three divisions were—the *villa urbana*, or dwelling of the proprietor ; the *villa agraria*, or dwelling for the labourers and the bestial required for the farm ; and the *villa fructuaria*, where the grain and other products were stored."

Applying these descriptions to the results of my excavations, it appears to me that the dwelling found under the Mound B may be considered as filling the conditions of a *villa urbana*. The careful way in which it had been built, its decoration, the fineness of its pottery, and the luxury implied by the whole facts, lead to this inference. Its communication with the Mound C (the baths) and with the Mound D (the *Lararium*) may also be considered as lending additional support to this view.

Comparatively few constructions have been discovered similar to that of the Mound D, and of some of these the destination is doubtful ; hence de Caumont classes them as " Temples incertaines," and recommends the further study of such edifices to all who explore Gallo-Roman remains. But I should be altogether at a loss to attribute to this building any other destination than that of a *Lararium*.

* *Ère gallo-romaine*, page 376.

The building under the Mound E may probably be regarded as the *villa agraria*. Its construction, as has been already stated, is inferior to that of the *villa urbana*, and there is neither decoration nor other evidence of luxury apparent in it. Some of the rooms, from their having plaster on the walls and concrete on the floors, may be presumed to have been inhabited by the labourers; others, destitute of these, would seem to have been used as stables and storehouses.

Remembering the persistence of names in Brittany, it may be observed that the field which adjoins this building on the west is named *Parc er poul* (the field of the waterpool). No pool of water exists there now, but it may have retained the name from its having been the *compluvium* for watering the bestial.

In the Mound F, the only portion of the building to which a destination could be assigned with certainty was the workshop of the smith. The fireplace, with cinders and scoriæ, the trough alongside of it, and the quantity of iron scattered about, left no doubt as to its object and use.

The ruins found under the Mounds G and H were so much dilapidated that no special destination could be certainly assigned to them. Seeing that the latter are situated so close to the entrance in the *enceinte*, it is possible that they may be the remains of a military post.

De Caumont, in speaking of *enceintes*, says[*]—" When the incursions of barbarians became frequent, I will ask if it was not necessary to have not only camps for the troops, but also places of refuge where the inhabitants of the country most exposed to being plundered could unite and place themselves under cover in the time of danger, and if this system of defence was not extended even to particular habitations. My

Ère gallo-romaine, page 613.

opinion is that many of the *enceintes* which are left to us were the enclosures of Gallo-Roman habitations, which from their importance were more exposed to pillage, and which could even serve as a place of refuge to the inhabitants of the surrounding country.   Thus there were, even from the fourth century, small towns and habitations fortified as in the Middle Ages."

It may be supposed that in the troublous times and disordered state of the country during the latter part of the Roman occupation some system of mural defence would have been then erected by the inhabitants of the Bossenno if they had not done so previously ; but the most of these have been destroyed by the tillage of the land.   On referring to the general plan the reader will see what is still left there which may be regarded as an *enceinte*.

From the exposed situation of the Bossenno, the inhabitants were exposed to attack, not only from enemies by land, but by sea also ; for, as has been already shown, the sea came close up to the Bossenno, and besides a landing in its vicinity could have been easily effected anywhere in the Bay of Quiberon.

Besides the ruins which my diggings have exposed, there must certainly have been numerous other constructions, both within and without the *enceintes*, possibly built with less care, and which have long ago disappeared.*   The clearing of the land for tillage has left no trace of these save in the names of the fields, and in the fragments of tiles and pottery strewn over their surfaces.   Thus, on referring to the general plan,

---

* The proprietors of the Bossenno adopted this view, and stated that they had not cleared away the mounds which I have excavated because the expense of doing so would have amounted to more than the value of the land.

there are two fields, Nos. 658 and 659, situated to the east of
the Mound B, which bear the significant names of *Helle-duen*
(the cinders) ; farther on are No. 727, *Ker-in-goh* (the old
town), No. 665, *Er goh fetan tal parc piard* (the old fountain
near the field of stones) ; and many others might be cited, not
only inside, but outside the *enceintes*.

About the year 1790 the mother of the present proprietor
of the Hôtel des Voyageurs at Carnac dwelt in the village of
Bomer, close to the Bossenno. She often spoke to her
daughter of having seen hollow bricks and a sort of conduit
which had been then discovered in working the fields of the
Bossenno. This discovery created much astonishment in the
country at the time, but no one attempted to follow it up.

The existence of the remains of buildings to the south
of the Bossenno has been already alluded to in the description of the Mound F. This shows that the town had
extended at least so far in that direction.

In an east and west direction it had extended from the
field Ker-in-goh to the foot of the Mont St. Michel, the
importance of which as a commanding point would not have
been overlooked by the Romans. This eminence (which will
be fully described in the following chapter) overlooks all the
surrounding country and the sea. It may be thus inferred
that it would be utilised as a post for observation. In fact
the levelling to which the top of the tumulus has been subjected has not altogether obliterated the traces of ancient
works ; and the occurrence of Roman tiles and pottery also
serves to bear out this inference.

Other Gallo-Roman ruins have been discovered about
200 yards to the south of this tumulus in the field named
Grah ba dou (heaps of debris). The following objects, which
have been found in this field of late years, are now deposited

in the Mairie of Carnac—viz., fragment of a statuette of the Venus Anadyomene; fragments of vases in fine red lustrous ware, and in grey and in black ware; a bronze axe, a waist buckle, and a coin of Alexander Severus.

All the fields on the south side of the Mont St. Michel are strewn with fragments of Gallo-Roman pottery, and the small cubic stones used in building by the Romans may be seen in the walls which form their boundaries.

The quantities of bones of ruminants and other animals, and numerous shells of edible molluscs everywhere found in these excavations, save in the Mounds D and H, supply the evidence of what had been the staple food of the inhabitants. Hunting and fishing would thus seem to have been largely practised, if we judge from the frequent recurrence of bones of the deer, hare, and rabbit, and from the remains of their fishing gear. Hunting scenes and animals running form a frequent ornamentation on the Gallo-Roman pottery found here, as they generally do on that found elsewhere.

The fact of so many bricks having been found bearing the prints of the feet of dogs which had passed over them in the soft state, shows that many of these animals had been kept, and the difference in the size of the prints also shows that they had been made by dogs of all sizes—from the small pet or lap-dog to the great watch-dog and hound.

The luxury of the table at Rome during the third century has been frequently described. Oysters were brought there from the Dardanelles, the Adriatic, and Armorica.[*] At present ostriculture forms a prominent industry in the Morbihan. Large sums have been expended on the oyster-

* Sunt et Aremorici qui laudant ostrea ponti.—AUSON. Ep. xiii. v. 35.

beds thus cultivated, which give employment to numerous hands, and their produce is regularly sold in Paris as *huîtres Armoricaines.*

Horace makes mention of snails as a stimulant to be taken with wine.[*] Pliny the younger alludes to them as having been served at table, although not so much esteemed as the oyster.[†]

On looking over the ceramics of the Bossenno we see that while some of the pottery is of a rude Celtic type, the greater portion is Gallo-Roman pottery, nearly all of which, I should be inclined to hold, had been made in Brittany. The Gallo-Roman potter had attained a high degree of excellence by adopting the Roman mode of working, while still preserving the ancient forms and the ornamentation characteristic of his country, viz. undulating lines and concentric circles. The leaves of aquatic plants and the figure of the sea-horse occur frequently among the fragments found. The hippocampus is still frequently caught by the fishermen in the Bay of Quiberon.

The Roman law obliged potters to put their trade mark or stamp on their products, but this does not seem to have been enforced in Gaul. Although all the bricks, tiles, and fragments of these found at the Bossenno were carefully examined for such stamps or names, not one was found. The only potters' marks discovered were on the two fragments of vases in the Mound E.

[*] Tostis marcentem squillis recreabis et Afra
　　　Potorem cochleæ.　　　　　　　　　HORACE, Lib. ii. Satire iv.

[†] Heu tu, promittis ad coenam, nec venis ! paratæ erant cochleæ ternæ.
. . . At tu apud nescio quem ostrea. . . maluisti. (Ep. i. xv.)

Great care was bestowed by the Romans on the manufacture of bricks and tiles. Vitruvius states that they sometimes remained two years drying in the shade, and that the firing occupied from fifteen to twenty days, with an extreme heat at the end. The bricks and tiles found at the Bossenno were in as good a state of preservation as if they had been freshly made. Roman tiles are found in the neighbourhood of Guerande, and are still occasionally used by the *paludiers* to close the water channels in the saltfields, in preference to modern tiles, which only last a few years.

The red lustrous ware called Samian is frequently alluded to by Roman authors, and has been found wherever the Roman dominions extended. It is supposed to have been made from B.C. 150 down to the fifth century of our era, and it has been proved, by the discovery of the potteries, to have been manufactured in several parts of France, amongst others on the right bank of the Allier. The red ferruginous earth necessary for its fabrication has been found in several parts of Brittany where there are potteries still. Brongniart mentions the magnificent glazing of this ware as the only one known to the ancients, and one which cannot now be produced. He describes it as being principally composed of a silicate, rendered fusible by the introduction of an alkali, such as potash or soda, and attributes the colour to a metallic oxide which had been either introduced into the composition or derived from the primitive paste.[*]

The same authority states[†] "that three modes of ornamentation were followed by the Roman potters :—1*st*, Moulding from single or from independent patterns representing the same or different subjects; 2*d*, The employment of

* *Traité des Arts Ceramiques*, tome 1, p. 545.　† *Ibid.* p. 424.

roulettes for forming circular zones on the circumference of
the vase, isolated ornaments being made by impressions from
a seal or stamp; 3*d*, The forming of an ornament in relief on
the vase, with slip flowing from a pipette," a method pecu-
liarly characteristic of Roman potteries.

Numerous examples of the first and second modes of
ornamentation were found in all the mounds.

It is somewhat significant that specimens of the third
mode of ornamentation were only found in the Mounds
A, B, C, and D. The chromo-lithograph A, Plate IV.,
represents a vase which had been ornamented by this curious
process.

In examining the objects in bronze, we find the two
civilisations, Gaulish and Roman, represented, as we have
just seen in the pottery; for whilst the two brooches (B, pl. III.
fig. 3 ; C, pl. XIII. fig. 3), and also most of the other bronze
ornaments, are of Celtic type, the coins are all Roman.

The curious statuette of an ox (E, pl. VI.), resembling the
bronze statuettes found in Egypt which have no disc between
the horns, recalls the fact, as the pottery did, that the Romans
had Moorish soldiers stationed at Vannes. Are we to attribute the statuette of the Mound E to the Egyptian mythology, to the Celtic mythology, or to the Mithraic worship ?
The worship of Mithras was introduced about the time of the
emperors at Rome, and thence spread over all parts of the
empire. The figure of an ox or bull frequently occurs on
Gaulish coins. In the Celtic mythology the two oxen of
Hu-Gadarn, a divinity of the ancient Bretons, are fabled to
have drawn out of the waters of the deluge, by means of
strong chains, the Avank, a monstrous crocodile which had
caused the submersion of the universe. This is alluded to in

one of the popular legendary ballads of Brittany, known by
the grotesque title of "The Frogs' Vespers,"* characterised
by Villemarqué as one of the most singular, and perhaps the
most ancient of Breton Ballads.   It consists of a dialogue
between a Druid and a child, in which a summary of the
Druidical mythology is given and recapitulated in a series of
twelve questions and answers.   The second of these is as
follows :—

> AR BUGEL :
> Kan d'in cuz a zaou ranu
> Ken a oufenn breman.
>
> ANN DROUIZ :
> Daou ejenn dioc'h eur gibi ;
> O sachat, o souheti.
> Edrec'hit aun estoni !

The Gaul of the Bossenno, in adopting the religion of his
conquerors, had not entirely abandoned his former deities.
The Gallo-Roman altar found under the cathedral of Notre
Dame at Paris has on two of its sides the Celtic divinity
Hesus and the Taurus trigaranus ; on the other two sides
the Roman divinities Jupiter and Vulcan.

It has been said of coins, that one of the most important
uses to which they can be applied, when the circumstance of
their discovery on a particular site is beyond question, is in
approximating dates.   The coins found at the Bossenno,
extending over the long space of one hundred and eighty-four
years—viz. from the third consulate of Marcus Aurelius to
the year three hundred and fifty-three, the epoch of the death
of Magnentius—thus bring us down to the middle of the
fourth century.

* *Barzas Breiz*, par le Vicomte H. de la Villemarqué.   Paris, 1867.

Historians are in accord as to the deplorable state of Gaul in the latter part of the fourth century, when its towns and villages were burned and pillaged, and its rural districts ravaged by invasions of barbarians both by sea and land. The population of the towns occupied themselves in constructing *enceintes* and walls of defence, not formerly needed, but now become of the first importance as an absolute necessity of existence.

While the country was weighed down by these misfortunes, the government, taking no steps to remedy them, only thought of collecting more taxes. Then, in the beginning of the fifth century, came the general rising, which took place in Armorica, against the Roman government, and it appears to me that it is to this epoch that the violent destruction of the Bossenno may be assigned.

In the beginning of the fifth century Christianity had made considerable progress in Armorica, but no trace or indication of it was found at the Bossenno. On the other hand, we have seen unequivocal evidences of paganism in the statuettes of Venus found in the Mounds A and D, and in the statuette of the ox found in the Mound E.

It may, perhaps, be surmised that, for some misdeeds, the pagan inhabitants of the Bossenno had been driven away, and that their habitations had been burned by their Christian neighbours, and, in so far, the legend of the Bossenno would be an echo of a forgotten event. That portion of the legend, however, which states that they were slain, is not borne out by the results of the excavations, for, among all the numerous bones collected, not a single fragment of a human bone occurred. This fact seems to indicate that the inhabitants had not been surprised and slain by those who destroyed their dwellings, but that they had found time to gain a refuge elsewhere.

In concluding these remarks on the excavations of the Bossenno, I may, perhaps, be permitted again to draw attention to the persistence with which legendary incidents and forms of ornamentation are transmitted in Brittany from generation to generation.   A striking example of the latter is given in the accompanying engraving.

CHALICE ENGRAVED ON A TOMBSTONE.

XI.

THE MONT ST. MICHEL.

L

THE MONT ST. MICHEL.

In the preceding chapter I have already alluded to the vestiges of Gallo-Roman constructions found on the flank of the Mont St. Michel. This eminence, from its commanding position, must have been an important dependence of the Bossenno, if only as a post for observation.

During the summer months of 1876 we could not work at the Bossenno until the crops were cleared off the fields, so the months of June and July were passed in making researches at the foot of the tumulus surmounting the Mont St. Michel, which yielded results different from those found at the Bossenno.

The Mont St. Michel is situated at the distance of half a mile to the east of the village of Carnac ; from its commanding position and peculiar form it stands out as a striking feature in the landscape, as seen from any point in the surrounding country.

It is the first resort of the tourists who arrive at Carnac, and they cannot make a better commencement in acquiring a knowledge of the country than by giving a short time to the examination of this hill, and of the fine panoramic view which is best seen from the summit of the tumulus.

Facing the south the view extends over the sea studded with islands and broken by promontories. On your left hand

you see Locmariaker, by some writers supposed to have been
Dariorigum ; farther on, in the same direction, the tumuli of
Arzon and Tumiac, excavated by the Polymathic Society, may
be made out with a telescope ; and still farther on the point of
St. Gildas de Rhuis brings up the memory of Abeilard.
Facing you are the islands of Houat and Hédic ; to the right-
hand Belle Isle, the largest of the islands of the gulf of the
Morbihan ; the promontory of Quiberon, the Fort Penthievre,
and isthmus leading to it, associated with the disastrous
landing of the *emigrés* in 1795. Turning to the right you
see the isle of Groix, the spires of Plouharnel, Erdeven, and
Etel.

Facing the north, the spires of Ploemel, Auray, Saint
Anne, Arradon, and Crach, are to be seen in the distance :
nearer at hand, and flanked by numerous dolmens, are the
three strange alignments of menhirs, or groups of gigantic
standing stones, viz. Ménec (the place of stones, or in another
rendering the place of remembrance) ; Kermario (the place
of the dead); and Ker-lescan (the place of burning.) Under
your feet almost, and to the right, are the Gallo-Roman ruins
of the Bossenno, and behind these the finely-wooded hill and
celebrated dolmen of Ker-Cado.

The base of the tumulus which surmounts the Mont St.
Michel forms an oval, measuring 400 feet in its major axis,
and 200 feet in its minor axis. The present height of the
tumulus above the crest of the hill is 33 feet, but it may be
supposed that it had been much higher in times previous to
the different levellings to which it has been subjected : very
possibly some of these may have occurred during the Roman
occupation, and certainly in later times, for the preparation of
the site of the chapel dedicated to St. Michael, which now
occupies part of the summit. Near the chapel stands a

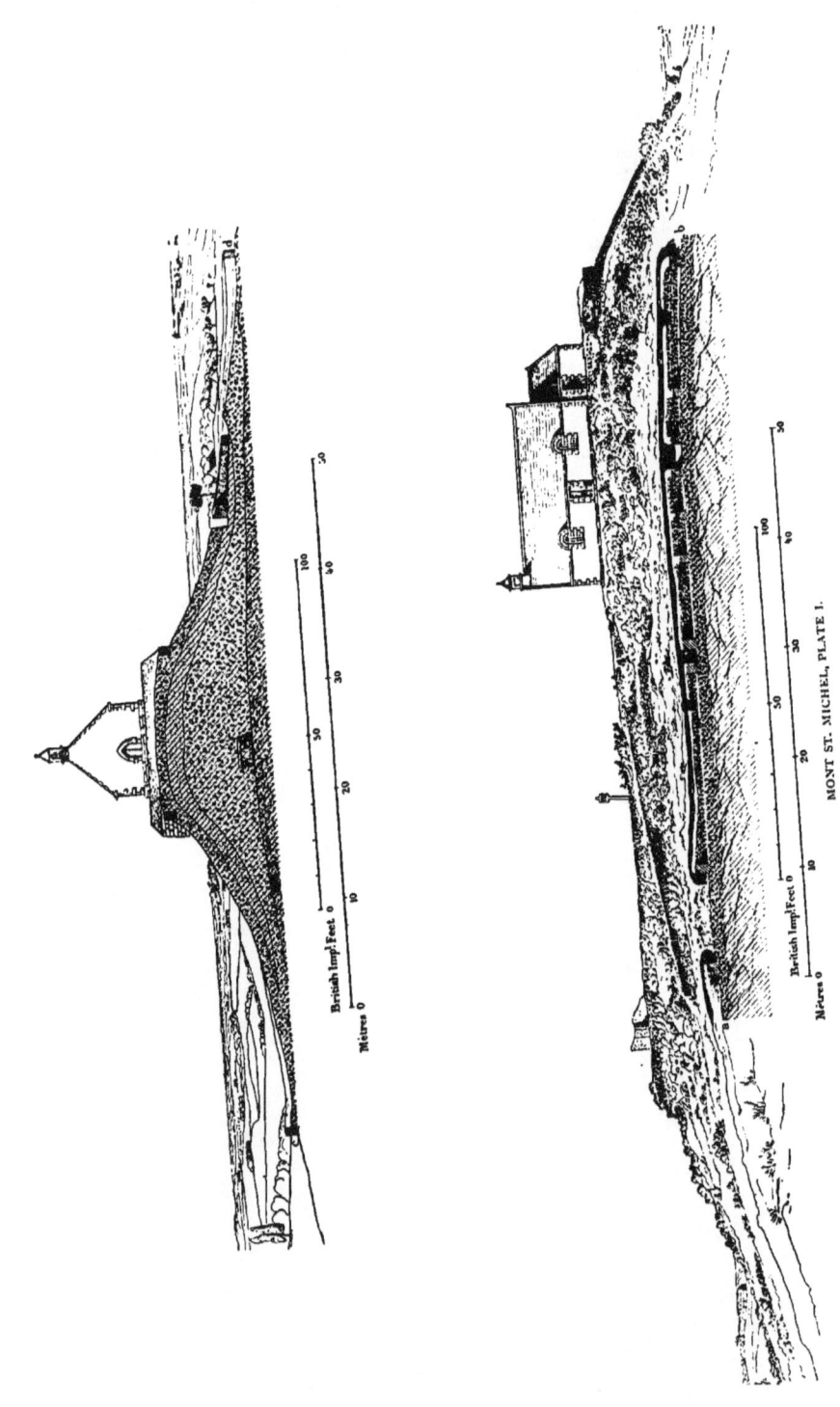

British Imp.l Feet 0

Mètres 0

British Imp.l Feet 0

Mètres 0

MONT ST. MICHEL, PLATE 1.

curious cross, rudely sculptured in granite.* At the west end of the summit are the ruins of a semaphore which was worked in the beginning of this century.

This tumulus is similar to the mounds of stones called in the Celtic *Carn*, in the lowland dialects cairn. Hence, it seems to me, is the origin of the name of the neighbouring village Carnac (the place of the carn), and this idea is strengthened by the name of the village at the foot of the hill, Cru-Carnac† (the rocky hill of the carn).

M. Rene Galles, in his report on the diggings of Mont St. Michel in September 1862, estimates that a mass of earth and stones equal to 40,000 cubic yards had been transported to the summit of this hill, the highest in the district, for the construction of the tumulus. I shall here quote a passage from the same report, which alludes to the construction of the tumulus, a view and section of which is shown in pl. I.

"With the view of facilitating our preparatory researches as much as possible, we marked on the platform of the tumulus the line of its major axis. A series of pits were next sunk from this line, which passed through a layer of stones for 2 feet 8 inches, and then came upon a bed of fine clay dried, and probably beaten hard. A similar envelope of fine clay has been found in the tombs which follow the line of the coast. This for a long time was regarded as composed of ashes. It had evidently been formed with the view of having a compact and solid covering over the mass of dry stones, so as to prevent the infiltration of rain-water. We determined by trials that along the summit the depth of this bed of fine

* See the figure at the end of this Chapter.

† The inhabitants call this village indifferently either Cru-Carnac or Clou-Carnac. In the ancient titles it is written Cru-Carnac.

clay was 5 feet 4 inches, and that below it a cairn of dry stones extended all along the tumulus.

" Having determined the situation of a point a little to the east of the centre of the tumulus, I commenced to sink a pit, having an orifice, measuring 3 feet 4 inches by 6 feet 8 inches, and which, according to our calculations, ought to pass very close to the chamber in the interior of the monument, the proximity of which would likely be indicated by some change in the aggregation of the heaped-up stones. *Near this place we expected from our levels to find the summit of the hill which supports the tumulus, is prolonged under it, and where we expected to find that the central chamber had been constructed.* This difficult work was performed by skilful workmen, who had been placed at our disposal by the kindness of the director of the tin-mines of La Ville-d'Er, for it was found necessary to take energetic measures to protect ourselves against the falling in of the heaped-up stones which rolled about us like lead shot in a sack."*

M. Rene Galles then goes on to state that at a depth of 26 feet 3 inches they came upon the chamber, and found therein eleven stone axes in jade, two large stone axes in a coarser material, twenty-six small stone axes in fibrolite, nine pendants, and one hundred and one beads ; some of which were in jasper, others in turquoise ; two flakes of flint, and a number of little beads formed of a sort of ivory. These objects are now exhibited in the Museum of the Polymathic Society of the Morbihan at Vannes.

One evening in the month of April 1875, when passing

---

* *Fouilles du Mont St. Michel en Carnac, faites en Septembre*, 1862, par Rene Galles, etc. Vannes, 3ᵉ edition.

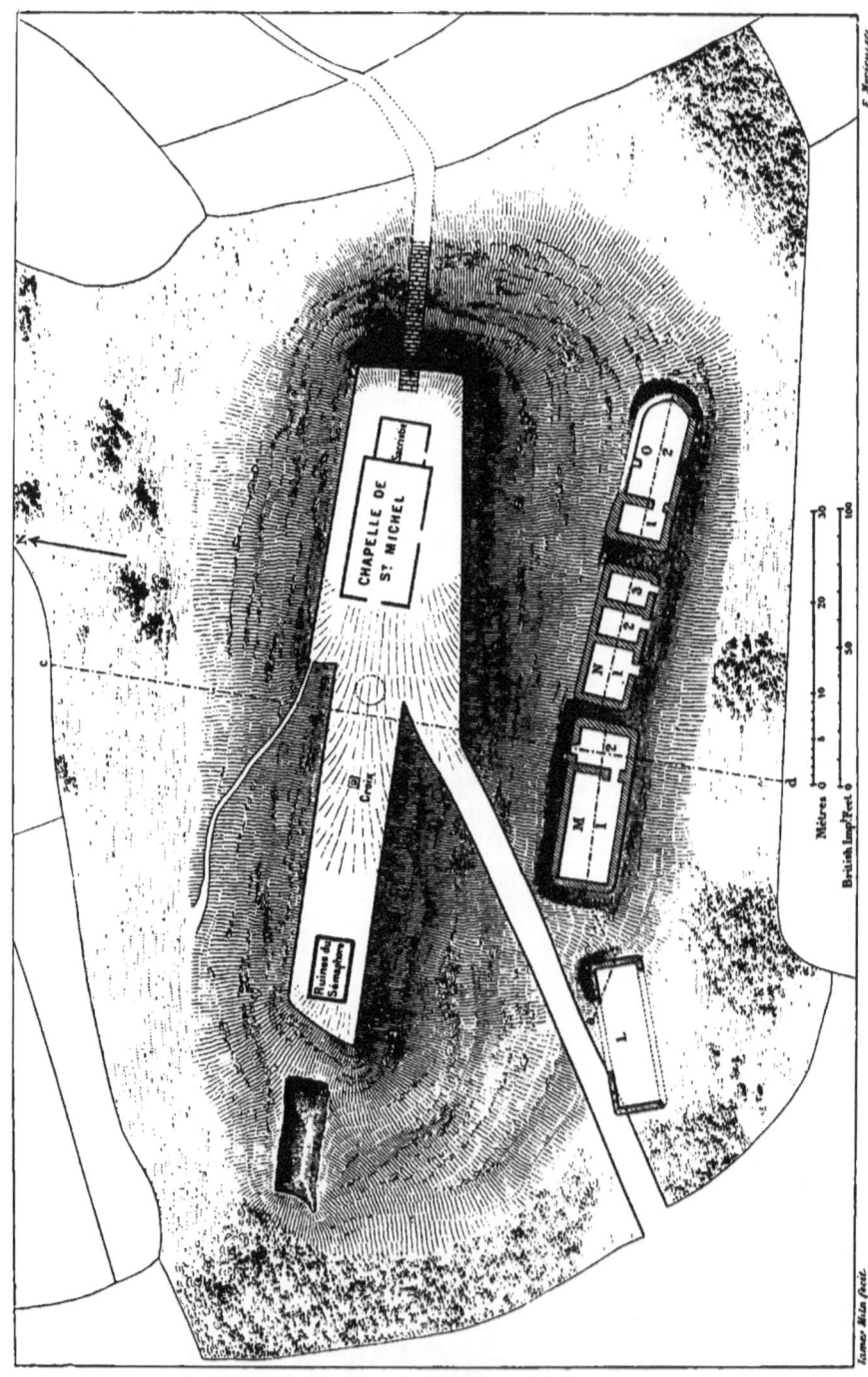

CHAPELLE DE ST. MICHEL

Sacristie

Ruines du Scriptorium

Croix

M
1
2

N
1
2
3

O
1
2

L

c

d

Mètres 0   5   10   20   30

British Imp. Feet 0   50   100

MONT ST. MICHEL, PLATE II.

James Akerman Lith.

E. Norway sc.

To face page 151.

along the south side of the tumulus, I remarked for the first time under the effect of a peculiar light some inequalities in the surface of the ground which surprised me, as I had so often passed there before without observing them. In poking amongst the grass with my walking-stick I struck upon some stones which appeared to be arranged in a line, and turned up some fragments of roofing-tiles (*tegulæ*) and Gallo-Roman pottery. A short inspection of the dry stone wall forming the demarcation of the adjoining fields showed that it contained numerous dressed stones. These indications made me resolve to prosecute some researches here so soon as time permitted and the necessary permission could be obtained.

We commenced these researches in the month of June 1876; the results were the discovery of four curious constructions running in an east and west direction, which are severally noted in the accompanying plan of the Mont. St. Michel by the letters L, M, N, and O.

We commenced by opening up the ground near the stones in line above mentioned, and soon found remains of dwellings.

The construction L, on being laid bare, was found to be of a rectangular form, measuring 54 feet in length by 17 feet in breadth. What remained of its walls had an average height of 2 feet, and 1 foot 8 inches in breadth.

The walls of this building, and also those of the constructions M, N, and O, were all rudely built of undressed stones, bound with a mortar of argillaceous earth, having the exterior but not the interior corners rounded off, and the courses of masonry, instead of being level, followed the slope of the hill. The extraction of building stone from a quarry cutting into the building L had destroyed the greater portion of it.

The following objects were found during the excavation of the construction L :—

Several fragments of roofing-tiles (*tegulæ*) near the surface of the soil.

Several pieces of grey schist, measuring 1 foot by 10 inches and half-an-inch thick, probably parts of roofing-slates.

Near the north-east angle a sufficient number of fragments were found to determine the greater part of the form of a vase rudely moulded by hand, and still bearing the marks of the potter's fingers all over it. It had a flat bottom and upright sides, the rim turned out at a right angle, the paste reddish-brown, coarse, with scales of talc visible, and badly fired. The diameter across the exterior of the rim is 2 inches, and across the interior 11 inches. A thick coating of soot on the surface indicates that it had been used for cooking. In one of the fragments of the bottom a band of iron was embedded, which had doubtless served to support it over the fireplace.

Several fragments of pottery in coarse yellow paste.

A few fragments of vases in a yellow paste, covered with a green vitreous glazing.

Four flakes of flint.

A small round bead in brick earth.

A four-sided whetstone, having a groove cut round the head, probably for suspension. (Mont St. Michel, pl. III. fig. 1, natural size.)

A whorl formed from a fragment of a vase in red paste, the perforation oblique and eccentric.

In clearing away the ground between the constructions M and N, the traces of fire, viz. ashes and charcoal, were found, and these were more strongly marked at the north-east corner of M, where we cut into the tumulus. It appears to me that these traces of fire had no connection with the buildings M

1

2

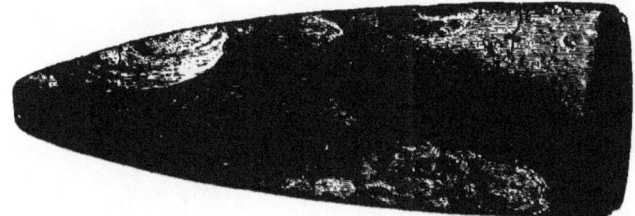

3

4   5

and N, but may be attributed to the time of the construction of the Tumulus.

The following objects were found here :

A flint knife. (Pl. III. fig. 2, natural size.)

A piece of iron measuring 6 inches in length, 4 inches in breadth and ½-inch thick, much oxidised ; use unknown.

Fragment of a curiously shaped vase, in a pale yellow paste, well fired, sonorous, covered with a light green vitreous glazing, and ornamented with a line of lozenge-shaped markings. (Pl. IV. fig. 3, natural size.) Pottery of this description is generally believed to be not earlier than the twelfth century.

In the centre of the large apartment No. 1 the fireplace was indicated by some stones embedded in the floor : these, reddened by the action of fire, were covered with a small quantity of charcoal and ashes, whilst around them were several flint flakes and shells of the limpet (*Patella vulgata*).

At the foot of the north wall we found :

A small fragment of a polished stone axe in diorite.

A piece of blue slate measuring 4 inches in length, 1½ inch in breadth, and ¼ inch in thickness ; rounded at one end and having polished edges.

A piece of vitrified scoriæ.

A small stone hammer of hemispheric form in grayish flint, 2 inches in diameter.

A spindle whorl in a brownish paste mixed with small grains of quartz, well fired, hollow on one face. (Pl. III. fig. 4, natural size.)

Fragment of the tibia of a ruminant.

Several fragments of pottery in a coarse brown paste,

covered with soot on the exterior, similar to the vase described in the building L.

Several fragments of very coarse pottery, some being in a yellow and others in a brown paste, badly fired.

Near the north-east corner, on the floor :

A nucleus or core of silex, from which flakes had been struck off.

Near the foot of the south wall :

A small fragment of fine thin glass.

A round piece of thin blue slate, having the edge cut smooth, 3 inches in diameter.

Several pieces of gray slate, perforated with holes $\frac{1}{3}$ inch in diameter, and very irregularly formed ; probably part of the roof of the building.

In the room No. 2, on the floor at the north-west corner :
Four flint flakes.

A small round piece of slate, smoothed, $\frac{3}{4}$ inch in diameter.

Several pieces of slate partly calcined.

On the floor of the doorway opening to the north :

A flake of flint and a fragment of a glass cup.

The building N, also of rectangular form, measures 50 feet in length by 22 feet in breadth. It is composed of three apartments of unequal dimensions, having no communication with each other, each apartment having a doorway giving access from the south. The walls and masonry are of the same description as those of the buildings L and M, and the floor is formed by a bed of argillaceous earth.

The room No. 1 measured 20 feet in length by 15 feet in breadth.

No. 2 measured 15 feet 8 inches by 10 feet.

No. 3   „   15 „ 8 „   „ 10 „   3 inches.

The following objects were found here :

In the room No. 1, on the floor, a flake of grayish flint.

Near the south-west corner :

A whorl, two inches in diameter, formed out of a fragment of a vase, in a yellowish red paste.

A small ball, in brick earth, ¾ inch in diameter.

A piece of red coarse pottery cut into a disc, 1 inch in diameter.

Near the south-east corner :

Fragments of vases of different forms, in yellow and grey pastes.

At the foot of the east wall :

Several fragments of a vase in a yellow paste, hard and sonorous, covered with a light green vitreous glazing, and ornamented with circular fluted bands.

Near the north wall :

Part of the tibia of a ruminant.

In the room No. 2, on the floor :

Three cores or *nuclei* in silex.

Fragments of a pestle in granite, 2¾ inches in diameter.

Two round stones in polished nephrite.

On the outside of the doorway of this room :

Several fragments of vases similar to that found in the building L.

Fragment of the rim of a plate of octagonal shape, having a rude ornament at each angle formed from the print of the potter's thumb.

In the room No. 3, on the floor:

One of a set of discs cut in granite, 2½ inches in diameter and ¾ inch thick.

An unfinished whorl formed from a piece of coarse red pottery, half perforated.

On the outside of the north wall, near the foot:

A few fragments of ridge tiles of a pale yellow paste, having an ornament on the upper part of diamond-shaped figures in relief.

The building O forms a parallelogram terminating in a hemicycle at the east end, measuring 51 feet in length by 22 feet in breadth. The walls are of unequal thickness, and in the north-east portion are merely blocked into the tumulus, and consequently there they have no exterior face. This also proves that the construction of this building was posterior to that of the tumulus. The average height and style of masonry are the same as in the preceding buildings.

The building O is divided into two rooms, the smaller of which, No. 1, measures 16 feet in length by 12 feet in breadth, and communicated with the room No. 2 by a doorway 5 feet 6 inches in width.

The room No. 2, measuring 36 feet 10 inches in length by 16 feet in breadth, has a doorway 5 feet 6 inches wide, giving access from the outside on the south side of the building. Opposite this doorway, and embedded in the floor at the foot of the north wall, is a dressed slab of granite measuring 3 feet in length by 1 foot 6 inches in breadth.

When commencing the excavation of this building a musket-ball was found near the surface of the ground, possibly a souvenir of 1815. At that time both the village of Carnac and the Mont St. Michel were held by the "Blues," when a strong party of "Chouans" arrived, and after a sharp skirmish gained possession of both these places.

The following objects were found during the excavation of this building.

In the room No. 1, on the floor :
Two pieces of flint.
Two discs made of brick tiles, 2 inches in diameter.
Half of a spindle whorl in brick paste, 1 inch in diameter.
Part of a horse-shoe, iron.
Two iron nails.
Several fragments of ridge tiles, the same as those found in the building N, and others having a line of oval-shaped ornaments on the top in relief.
Two teeth of the pig.
Knee-cap bone, and part of the thigh-bone of a ruminant.

In the room No. 2, on the floor :—
Several slates $\frac{1}{8}$ inch in thickness, perhaps part of the roof of the building.
Two discs formed of brick tile $1\frac{1}{2}$ inch in diameter.
Small round piece of slate $\frac{2}{3}$ inch in diameter, having the figure of a cross incised.
Fragment of a glass cup thin and clear.
A considerable quantity of fragments of coarse brownish-red earthenware.
Fragment of a plate of an octagonal shape, in a gray-brown paste, having an ornament at the angles formed by the print of the potter's thumb.

Fragment of a vase in a yellow paste, having a band of oval-shaped ornaments in relief, formed by the print of the potter's fingers. (Pl. IV. fig. 4, natural size.)

Several fragments of a vase in a yellow-red paste, having thin sides and the rim turned inwards. One of the fragments is riveted with brass wire.

The neck, handle, and other fragments of a vase in a yellow paste, of the form of a water bottle, pierced with a number of small holes. (Pl. IV. figs. 1 and 2, natural size.) Similar pottery was found in the Mound D.

Two fragments of a plate in yellow earth covered with a green vitreous glazing, and having a collar round the rim.

Bottom of a small vase 2¼ inches in diameter, in a red paste, and covered in the interior with a vitreous glazing of a light green colour.

A large quantity of fragments of coarse pottery in yellow and in gray paste.

Near the north-west corner were the traces of a fireplace, ashes, charcoal, and shells of the limpet (*Patella vulgata*).

At the foot of the north wall :—

Several fragments of slate having an ornament formed by incised lines rudely cut in squares and lozenges.

In the trench cut outside the semicircular termination, at the depth of 3 feet 4 inches :

A polished stone axe in white flint, which seemed to have undergone the action of fire. (Pl. III. fig. 3, natural size.)

In taking a general survey of these ruins, and the objects found in them, there arises a difficulty in the want of sufficient data, which prevents any exact conclusion as to their date. The evidence of the ruins is only of a negative character; no tradition exists about them, no document mentions them, and

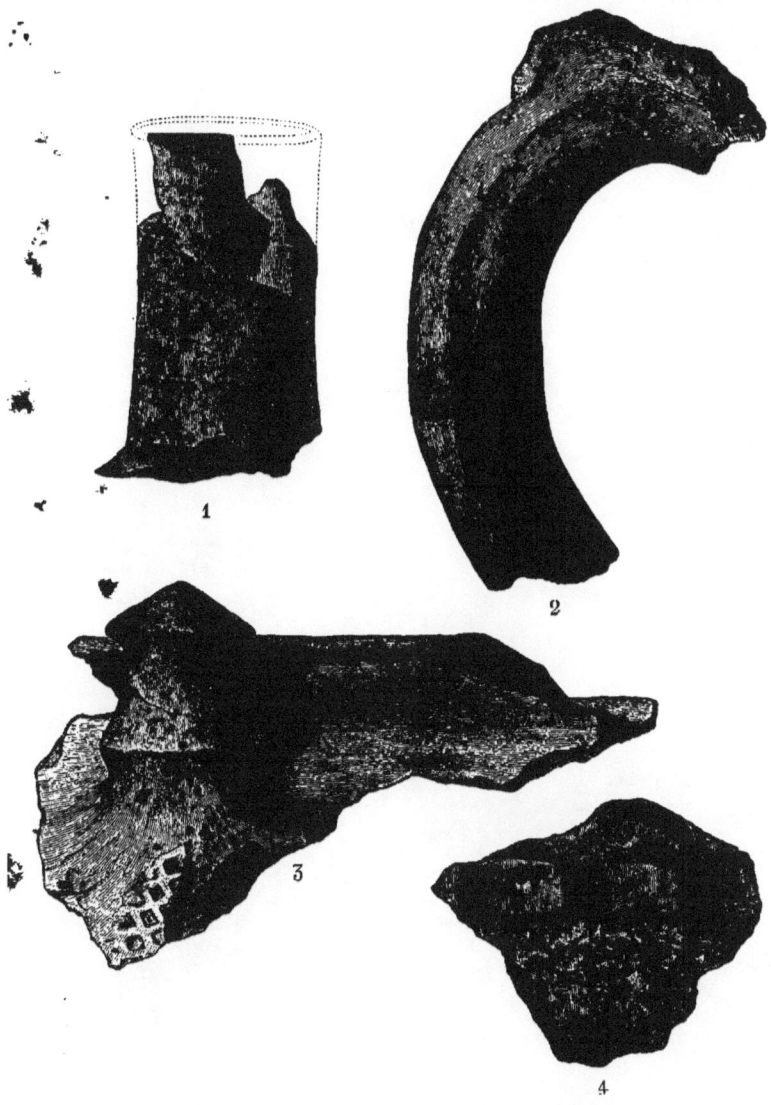

1

2

3

4

so far as I can ascertain they were entirely unknown in the country before the excavations just described brought them to light.

At the Bossenno we had the remains of houses carefully and well built in regular courses of small cubic stones, the walls richly ornamented, and floors covered with cement. Here the constructions are in rough irregular masonry, the walls are destitute of plaster, and the floors of cement. They are evidently not Gallo-Roman. But the fragments of Roman tiles and pottery found on the tumulus, and the small cubic building stones in the wall of the adjacent field, all indicate that there must have been a Roman or Gallo-Roman construction hereabouts, probably at a period anterior to that of the ruins.

The rude masonry, the rounding off at the corners, the hearth in the middle of the floor,—all of these forcibly remind one of the ancient form of rudely built dwellings still constructed in the Hebrides.

In cutting below the floors of the constructions M, N, and O, we came upon the bed of fine clay which has been already mentioned as covering the tumulus, then the wall of the building was in part blocked into the tumulus. These facts are sufficient to show that the buildings were erected subsequently to the construction of the tumulus.

The objects found in and about these buildings belong to epochs so very different, that inferences drawn from them are necessarily conflicting. It appears to me that there is no connection between these buildings and the stone implements found outside their walls, which may be classed with the date of the sepulchral rites before the elevation of the tumulus.

Some of the pottery collected in these buildings may be

classed as of Celtic type, but alongside of these fragments were some belonging to the Middle Ages, and others which cannot be dated before the seventeenth century.

The ruins may thus perhaps be the remains of one of the primitive monastic establishments which were founded by the emigrants from Great Britain, on their arrival in Armorica. Under that hypothesis the building O would have been the church of the convent; its form and size are similar to the primitive Christian churches in Brittany. On the other hand, these buildings, after having been abandoned by the brotherhood, may have been occupied up to a comparatively modern time by men of different generations who have left the traces of their occupation behind them.

De Caumont states in his *Architecture Religieuse* that the primitive Christian churches were copied from the Roman basilicas, which served the double purpose of tribunals and commercial exchanges.

One of the oldest constructions which remains in Brittany is the chapel of St. Agatha, in the department of Ile et

GROUND-PLAN OF CHAPEL OF ST. AGATHA.

Vilaine. It is situated close to the parish church of Langon, about a mile from the railway station of Fougeray Langon, on the line between Rennes and Redon. The general form

of this chapel is that of the ancient basilicas. The nave
measures 26 feet 3 inches in length by 12 feet in breadth.
The apse or hemicycle at the east end measures 6 feet 7
inches by 12 feet. The walls are of Roman work built with
small cubic stones, averaging $3\frac{1}{2}$ inches of a side, and having
the courses separated by a layer of lime mortar $\frac{3}{4}$ of an inch
in thickness. These courses are regulated at intervals by
double rows of long bricks. The entrance, which is from the
south, is covered by a Roman arch, which seems, however, to
be of more recent *construction* than the body of the church.
The windows are very small, and, from their destroying the
uniformity of the masonry, appear to have been inserted after
the erection of the building. These are four in number, one
in the apse, two in the north wall, and one in the front. A
few years ago, on removing from the vault of the apse a thick
coat of plaster covered with the rude painting of the Middle
Ages, there was discovered the most curious fresco-painting
which the Romans have left in Brittany. It represents
Venus rising from a blue sea, surrounded with fishes, among
which is a dolphin playing.

This chapel is mentioned in a charter of the twelfth
century as *Ecclesia Sancti Veneris*. The patron of Pluvigner
near Auray is Saint Vener, or Vigner. The chapel of St.
Agatha must have been erected originally as a Gallo-Roman
temple of Venus, and afterwards dedicated to a saint bearing
a similar name. The Breton name for Venus is *Vener*.
Gregoire de Rostrennen gives it as *Wener, Vener, Guener.*[*]

This superposition of constructions of so different a nature
on the Mont St. Michel is the very history of Brittany, where
at every point you meet with traces of three great periods

[*] *Dictionnaire François-Celtique seu François-Breton*, par le P. F. Gregoire
de Rostrennen. Rennes, 1732.

M

confused together in the minds of the people—viz. the period of the stone monuments, usually called Celtic; the period of the Roman domination; and the Christian period. The carn or tumulus was erected on the hill; then came Roman constructions; and, lastly, the Christian Church and cross which now crown the summit of the tumulus.

CROSS ON THE MONT ST. MICHEL.

www.ingramcontent.com/pod-product-compliance
Lightning Source LLC
Chambersburg PA
CBHW020848020726
47497CB00005B/1315